J.P. CHOQUETTE

Writers' Retreat

Contents

Acknowledgement

Many, many thanks to stellar early reader, Erin Chagnon, who is part editor, part proofreader, part genius. And to my editor, Emily Clark. Your hard work is much appreciated. Any leftover typos are my own.

Thanks to you too, dear reader. I am fortunate to have you read and enjoy my work and recommend it to others.

To my family and friends, thank you for your continued support. And most of all, thank you to God, for giving me any writing talent I possess.

~Dios Amore

Also By J.P. Choquette

Monsters in the Green Mountains series
　　Stillwater Lake
　　The Pact
　　Under the Mountain
　　Shadow in the Woods
　　Silence in the Woods

Tayt Waters Mystery series
　　See No Evil
　　Hear No Evil

Stand-alone books
　　Let the Dead Rest
　　Dark Circle
　　Epidemic

Prologue

Legs like leaden bars, I stumbled over a small, downed birch tree. My foot caught a broken branch and I pitched forward. Arms outstretched instinctively to break my fall, my hands landed in the mud. When I stood again I was dizzy with fear.

The wind blew hard, a sudden gust that shook the trees nearest me, rattled the branches.

A wise old owl lived in an oak. The words from the childhood rhyme spun through my mind unbidden. *The more he saw the less he spoke. The less he spoke the more he heard.* What was the last line, I wondered dully.

". . . out!" The voice behind me was louder. Closer. What had it said? Get out?

No. Spread out.

I pulled myself up. Forced my feet forward. *Please, let a car come now. Please, please, please.*

The end of the rhyme came suddenly to mind. *The more he saw the less he spoke . . .*

I'd never liked it. Goosebumps had run down my back and made me look twice, three times under the bed before launching myself into it. Trying not to touch the floor where the dark strip of emptiness lay.

I wobbled on shaky legs.

Run. I commanded myself. *Run.*

But all I could do was shuffle. My body was spent, energy gone. I shook so hard that the woods around me vibrated.

Ahead of me, through a tangle of vines smothering branches though, I saw something.

Headlights.

The road ahead stretched out like a river, undulating downhill. At the bottom of the hill, twin lights pointed in our direction. A beacon calling to me.

My legs were so heavy. I stumbled toward the lights. Toward safety. It wasn't that far. Just over the knoll and down the road a little further. Hope fluttered against my aching ribs. It wasn't far. I was nearly—

Hands clamped onto my shoulders. Such a hard grip, digging into me. Off balance, I pitched forward. Tried to scream as I connected with the ground. All that came out was a tiny whimper.

"Get over here," the voice was stern. The hard hands jerked my arms behind me. Roughly, so that something in my back popped. I whimpered, wanting to scream but couldn't find the strength. Gravel pressed against my cheek, damp from tears.

The last line of the nursery rhyme came to me then. *Why can't we all be like that wise old bird?*

Chapter One

Before

I peered out of the rain-slicked windshield and frowned. I'd lost cell service forty minutes earlier. Still, my cellphone had announced Idyll Weiss Retreat Center was eight hundred feet ahead.

My body ached from hunching over the steering wheel. My legs felt twitchy, and I wanted to get out, stretch, stop driving. But the wipers flew across the glass, barely keeping up with the torrent of rain hitting it. I squinted again and tried to see through the gloominess. The landscape around me was stark and dismal. Black tree branches poked up at the sky like accusing fingers, while a carpet of dead leaves lay in wet heaps over the ground. The road had turned to dirt and was narrow. If another car came from the opposite direction, I wasn't sure what I'd do—with a steep drop on my right, and little room on the left, it'd make the road impassable for both vehicles.

I'd passed through a small town—*town* being a generous description—ten minutes before.

"Okay, it looks like the road should be on your left coming up." Speaking out loud had always made me feel less alone, less anxious. And there was plenty to be anxious about. I glanced at the steep ravine bordering the road. The guardrails were rusted and in one place nearly caved in. My hands, already clenching the wheel, tightened.

"Arrived." The GPS announced.

Seconds later, I let out a shaky breath, relieved when a handmade wooden sign with the words Idyll Weiss painted in curling script greeted me. I slowed the car enough to make the sharp turn onto an even narrower driveway. A large boulder lay directly across from it.

Taking one hand at a time off the steering wheel, I dried it over my jean-clad legs, forced myself to take a couple of deep breaths. This trip was a test in more ways than one. Two years ago, I'd never have believed I could do this. Not only the writers' retreat—being in a strange, secluded place with strangers—but driving here myself. And in a rainstorm no less. Not after—

No.

Not here; not now.

I shoved the thought roughly to the cobwebby dark place in my mind.

Putting out a hand, I made a smeary pass over the foggy windshield, carving a spot to see more clearly through. I was about to give up hope that I'd ever arrive when a small parking area came into view. It was empty. I pulled into it and sank back in my seat, turning off the car. Rain thumped hard on the roof. I'd been driving so long that behind my eyelids I saw only more road stretching out before me.

In the application packet, it had been "highly recommended" that guests leave their vehicles behind to "help protect the environment." Since the retreat was only available to Vermonters, there were carpool areas in the largest cities in the northern and southern parts of the state. The retreat leaders would meet guests at one of these locations and we'd take one vehicle to the center.

I'd toyed with the idea. But in the end, I knew I had to do this. Driving here on my own was a test that I needed to pass. After what had happened, I never thought I could do this. But I had. I'd come—

Bang! Bang!

Jumping, I half-screamed. Something had hit the window near me.

A dripping, dark figure stood beside the car. It loomed closer. Instinctively, I jerked back toward the passenger seat. Then a bright beam of light pointed upward. A pink, potato-like face shone out from inside the jacket's hood.

"You must be Flora," the woman yelled.

I nodded, then cracked open the window. Rain zinged in like tiny darts. "Yes." My heart banged hard into my ribs.

"I've been waiting for you. This way." She motioned for me to follow. "I'm Ruby Keller. We talked on the phone." Her voice was reedy in the strong wind.

I nodded, then realized she might not be able to see me in the darkness of the car's interior.

"This way," she said again and pointed to a little muddy trail I could barely see in the gloom.

Wishing I had an umbrella, I grabbed my raincoat from the backseat and struggled into it. When I got out, rain immediately soaked every part of me that wasn't covered by the jacket. Hurrying, I opened the back door to get my bag. Ruby grabbed it from me. I jerked back, startled, then saw her grin.

"Customer service," she yelled, motioning toward the car.

"Need anything else?"

I retrieved my phone and purse, leaving the map, water bottle, and a granola bar wrapper where they were.

"Let's get out of this rain." She started toward the path.

I glanced back once before the trees and undergrowth swallowed us up. My car looked dejected. Its foggy windows peered back at me like cloudy eyes.

It was raining too hard to talk. Instead, I tried to keep up with Ruby's brisk pace. She must be in her seventies, but I struggled to keep up. Wet branches slapped at my jacket and face. When I pushed them away the icy rain ran in rivulets down my arms. My shoes were quickly drenched, and I suspected, muddy, though it was too dark for me to see.

We walked for at least five minutes. I was about to yell to Ruby and ask how much further when she stopped abruptly. I banged into her back, and she made a little *oomph* sound.

"Sorry."

She pointed ahead of us. "Straight ahead. Come on, come on. Let's get you out of this wet."

At first, I couldn't see what she'd pointed to. Then the hulking shadow of the house was visible. It was strangely constructed, with jutting sections coming off the main one as though an afterthought. It looked stone and about three centuries old. A buttery-yellow glow came from the windows on the bottom floor though and relief flooded me. I followed Ruby under the overhang on the small front porch.

"Welcome to Idyll Weise," she said proudly and threw her arms open. Her hood fell back as she did and her hair—a mix of yellow and gray—shone in the light coming from inside the building.

"Built in the year of our forefathers . . . or something like that," she laughed, a surprisingly girlish sound. "It was modeled after the country house of Marie Antoinette in Versailles." She removed her coat and shook the rain off. I followed suit.

"You're our last arrival. The others are anxious to meet you."

I wondered how long she'd been standing out there in the rain waiting for me.

I smiled and tried to ignore the cold, wetness morphing from my skin into my bones.

"I'm looking forward to meeting them too," I responded automatically. Though not as much as I was to find dry clothes and change.

"You must be cold. Let's get you warmed up and get some hot tea in you. You'll feel better in no time."

I hung my dripping jacket next to hers under the overhang. I was about to thank her when she opened the door and grabbed my arm. The feeling of her wet hands was like a cold fish on the back of my bicep, and I had to force myself not to shake off her grip as she propelled me into an entryway. We followed a short hallway that emptied into a room with a large fieldstone fireplace. It took up at least half the wall and was nearly as tall as me.

"There," she motioned me closer to the fire which roared in the grate. "Stand there for a moment and dry yourself. I'll get a towel and some hot tea."

I let my bag *thunk* to the floor and held out my hands to the fire. The warmth was comforting. As I rubbed my hands together, I looked around the room. It was large, a few ugly antique chairs dotted the space, one of them a rocker. A couple of mismatched end tables were the only other furniture. It was hard to deduce the room's purpose. A giant, black hook snaked out over the fire, but nothing was hanging from it. The stones on the chimney above the grate were blackened, but flickering light from the flames made it look like there were letters carved into the stone. I moved closer. There were letters there, words that I couldn't make out. I leaned closer, tried to get a better look. "Let all who . . ." something illegible ". . . leave renewed." Hmm, Nice sentiment for a Retreat Center. Though this didn't look like any retreat center I'd ever seen advertised.

The center didn't have a website, but the brochure I'd found at a natural foods store had boasted "a remote country retreat without modern distractions." It had also made it clear that the retreats were small—only a handful of writers—rustic, and intense.

It wasn't until weeks later after my application had been received and approved, that I learned Venetia Valentine was one of the retreat's founders. The name had sent a thrill through me. Venetia Valentine was the J.K. Rowling or Stephen King of the literary fiction world. Her books had won award after award, her name splashed across the fronts of writing magazines and some of the biggest writing conferences in the industry years ago. Then, suddenly, she'd dropped out of sight and off the public's radar.

There had been years of speculation—everything from cancer treatments to U.F.O abductions to a mental breakdown. But Venetia herself had maintained a radio silence. I'd found only two clips of her in recent years. One featured a group of rabid paparazzi trailing her from her flight to a waiting car at the JFK airport. A single image accompanied the swarm. Venetia with her hand out in front of her face, deflecting the blaze of flash bulbs.

The second didn't have a picture. It had been a short article in a national writing magazine—the only one I subscribed to—with a sort of writers' roundup. "Where Are They Now?" the headline had queried. It featured five well-known authors who'd stopped writing. Venetia had been featured as the third writer in the piece. Third! The journalist had posed a different question to each writer featured. To Venetia, he'd asked if there were any regrets in giving up her writing career. She'd told him that she was doing something bigger, more important now. Healing from her past and making a new future for herself. She had moved to New England, to a house in the woods where she planned to create a "sanctuary for writers." Those were the exact words she'd used. They'd stuck with me all these years.

The fire snapped and I turned to warm my back. The light in the hallway flickered and I realized it was coming from lanterns, not electric lights.

The room I stood in had no lights at all, the large fire casting enough of a glow to ward off all but the deepest shadows in the corners. The brochure had featured a handful of pictures of the outside spaces—a clear-blue pond framed with trees, a bench swing, and a small, whitewashed building tucked into a grove of pine trees—but not many of the Retreat Center itself. None of its interior. It had described Idyll Weiss as *rustic*. I'd assumed it had meant minimalistic décor, roughhewn beams, and lots of tartan blankets tossed over couches.

I hadn't expected this.

"Here we are," Ruby swung through a side door with a steaming pot on a tray, a thick stoneware mug, and a towel draped over her arm.

"You can use this first." She handed me the towel after depositing the tea tray on one of the small tables.

"Quickly now, you don't want to miss out on the introductory session. It's where you'll learn about all the ins and outs of the house and grounds. And meet the other writers and instructors."

"Will Venetia be there?" The towel was rough and dry in my hands. When I started wiping my hair with it, I caught the scent of camphor. A memory of Nona came to mind, her humming over me as I lay coughing on her scratchy brown couch.

"She will." Ruby smiled, grabbed my bag, and opened it. "Now, let's see."

I stared at her, startled.

She started to paw through my things.

"What are you doing?"

"Getting you some dry clothes." She glanced up with an expression of disbelief on her face. "What did you think I was doing?"

"Oh, um. No, thank you." My stomach clenched. "I'll change later." I moved to take the bag from her.

She held onto it firmly. "You don't want to catch a cold. Do it now, here by the fire where it's warm." A smile wreathed her pink face. "Don't worry, I've seen it all many times before."

I fought back a laugh. Did she expect me to strip in front of her?

"I'm fine."

My teeth were nearly chattering but I wasn't going to admit that to her. Instead, I grabbed the bag from her, pushed my things back into it, and zipped it shut.

Ruby shrugged. "Suit yourself."

Her voice was still pleasant, but a red tinge had crept up her neck. "Have some tea at least."

She stood and poured me a mug of steaming brown liquid, not making eye contact as she handed it to me.

The mug was scalding hot. I gasped and nearly dropped it.

"Careful, it's hot." She glanced at me. A little smile had formed around the corners of her mouth. "Bring it with you to the introductory session. I can take your bag to your room now. Or you can leave it here and take it up afterward."

I hesitated. I didn't want to leave it anywhere near her.

"Thanks, but I'll bring it with me."

"Suit yourself," she said again. Her tone was decidedly less friendly. She turned abruptly and walked through a different door on the opposite side of the room. Juggling both my bag and purse, I thought of leaving the tea behind but the prospect of something hot inside of me was too tempting. I wrapped the corner of the towel around its scalding sides and followed.

Chapter Two

I followed Ruby down a cramped, dark hallway stuffed with books from floor to ceiling. A single lantern hung along the bookcases, its shadowy flame casting strange movements on the walls. The titles were impossible to read, but the books looked very old. The hallway was slightly musty.

Ruby stopped suddenly and I nearly ran into her. I clutched the heavy mug so I wouldn't spill hot tea on Ruby or me.

Well, mostly me.

Ruby used both hands to push open a heavy-looking oak door. It swung silently open. Beyond it was a medium-sized room. A big, hand-hewn table dominated the space. More lanterns on the walls filled it with a warm glow. Faces swiveled in our direction, but I was distracted by the massive sculpture hanging from the ceiling. It was made entirely of antlers of all sizes and shapes. Huge moose antlers mixed with all types of deer and maybe sheep or mountain goat horns too. They were jumbled together in a cacophony of sharp edges. It was hideous and lovely at the same time.

Someone in the room cleared their throat and I blinked, glanced around the room.

"Sorry for the interruption," Ruby's voice was soft and her face serene. "This is our last guest, Flora Rossi."

The faces around the table smiled and I did too, automatically. I shifted the weight of my bag which started to slide from my shoulder. The hand holding the tea shook slightly, the angle of my wrist twisted and awkward.

"Welcome, Flora. Please, sit."

And then I realized who'd just spoken to me. Venetia Valentine. *The* Venetia Valentine. I'd memorized sections of her sharp, painfully beautiful prose. I slipped into the empty chair closest to me, struggling to stuff my bag under the table while balancing my mug of tea. The man to my right hefted it under in one smooth motion and I murmured a thank you.

Venetia's books had been so popular, lines had formed the night before a release. I'd been in them twice, camping out until the shop opened—two hours early—for hungry readers to pour through its doors. She'd won a Pulitzer along with many other awards that made other writers give a little sigh of *What if?* when mentioned.

I couldn't believe I was here. In the same room as her.

Her eyes bored into me from across the wide expanse of table. "We were just going over a few of the housekeeping details. I'm Venetia, one of the leaders here."

I nodded, embarrassed by how starstruck I was.

"Uh, thank you. Sorry for the interruption. And for being late. The rain—"

Another woman with short graying brown hair made a *tsking* sound in her throat and moved toward me.

"One more reason you should have carpooled," she muttered, putting a small burlap coaster under my mug.

"This table is an antique, as is much of the furniture and décor here at the Retreat Center," Venetia said. "Paula is adamant that we respect our surroundings. She'll offer reminders throughout your time here. We're fortunate to have such dedication, aren't we?" Venetia smiled benignly, but heat had climbed into my cheeks. I felt instantly transported to third grade, where mean Mrs. Till had taken special delight in embarrassing her clumsier students. Of which I topped the list.

"Now, let's go over the lay of the land, as it were. We'll go through introductions again at the end for the benefit of our newest arrival . . . and for those of us whose memory isn't quite as it used to be."

I listened to her speak but my mind was trying to match up this new version of Venetia compared to the publicity photos from past book tours and author events. Then, she'd had medium-length dark hair, with a slender frame, perfect makeup, and a stylish wardrobe. Now, she was graying, her hair long, falling in loose waves down her back. Her face was devoid of makeup, and she wore a sack-like blue dress that reminded me of a nightgown. She'd gained weight, though, on her tall frame, it looked healthy. Her eyes though, as they swept over us were the same. Arresting. Intense. Intelligent.

"As was mentioned in the welcome packets you received earlier this week, there is no electricity here at Idyll Weiss. We use a combination of oil lanterns and candles in the common areas. You'll each be given a lantern to use during your time here, which should be kept in your rooms when not in use. Of course, you're welcome to use flashlights. We have some in a basket near the door," she nodded toward the entrance, "that you can use during your stay. Paula will give you a quick tutorial on how to use your lantern safely while you're with us as well. This is a very old building. We don't want any accidents.

"Your laptops won't be much good as you won't be able to charge them. But, I always think that plain paper is much better for the type of deep work we'll be doing while you're here anyway.

"Additionally, we have shall we say," she cleared her throat. "Primitive plumbing. We do have running water—there's a hand pump in the kitchen—but the privies are located outdoors. Again, Paula will show you these on the tour following our session here."

I shivered, half from the cold, wet clothes sticking to me and half from what Venetia had just said. This was beyond *rustic*. Privies? No electricity? I'd assumed we'd be spending seven days without Wi-Fi. How had I missed those details in the welcome packet? The week had been a whirlwind though—a sudden cold had put me out of commission for a few days which had put me behind on my writing deadlines. The truth was, I'd barely skimmed the welcome packet while tossing clothes into my bag.

I gave myself a mental shake. This was going to be good for me. Away from the hustle and bustle of everyday life. The quiet would give me the perfect opportunity to focus on my book. Finally get it finished. I'd been camping. Once. Surely this was an upgrade from that.

The guy who'd helped me with my bag cleared his throat and raised his hand halfway.

"Let's hold all questions until the end." Venetia went on dispersing information.

Meals were taken at seven, twelve, and seven and had to be eaten in the dining room or outdoors. There were no exceptions to this rule and absolutely no food allowed in bedrooms.

"It could cause an infestation," she said. No one asked what of.

The overarching goal of the Idyll Weiss Retreat Center, Venetia said, was to provide us writers—who wrote in different genres—to reconnect with our muses, to enjoy the restoration and relaxation that the Retreat Center offered, and, perhaps, most importantly, to distance ourselves completely from the outside world. In addition to the classes, we'd have one-on-one intensive sessions with Venetia. Something squeezed in my chest at this information—excitement or fear?—but I tucked it away as she covered other details of our stay.

We were responsible for maintaining our bedrooms—there was no housekeeping service here. Much of the food came from the animals and gardens at the Retreat Center, organic of course. Herbal walks could be led by request. We were welcome to explore the outdoors—in fact, it was highly recommended—but Venetia asked that we remain on the paths and only go into the outbuildings if accompanied by an instructor, for insurance reasons.

Daily meditation and yoga sessions were led by the instructors. There was a schedule of these in our packets. There was a single phone in Venetia's office. It was only to be used for emergencies.

"Forget about social media, who is doing what with whom, where your friends or coworkers are having lunch or what they're doing in their free time this week. Embrace this chance to connect with your creative spirit." Venetia's eyes bored into us as she looked around the table. "We've found that this can best be done in an environment where distraction is limited."

I'd assumed because of the remoteness of Idyll Weiss; I wouldn't be able to use my cell phone. The thought had filled me with both elation and dread. Honesty, a week away from the online world didn't seem such a steep price to pay if it helped my muse come out of hiding.

There would be group sessions each morning and afternoon following breakfast and lunch, Venetia said. The later parts of the afternoon were meant to be spent on our own: writing in our rooms, any of the common areas, or outdoors. There was a beautiful pond nearby where we'd find swings and smooth banks perfect for sitting and dreaming.

"Lastly, on behalf of all of us, I welcome you to Idyll Weiss. This is your home for the next week. We hope you'll feel seen, valued, and heard while here. We also ask that you be respectful—to yourself, to each other, and of each of the instructors. Remember that this is our permanent home. We ask that you respect our privacy. No photos. And no entering any spaces marked private."

Venetia's gaze trailed around the circle of writers at the table, making eye contact with each one.

"November in Vermont isn't the most beautiful month," Venetia smiled. "But it is perfect for a cozy writing retreat, isn't it?"

Chuckles came from around the table as I tested my mug of tea. It had finally cooled down enough for me to cup my hands around it. I sighed unintentionally. Just hearing about the property and places to write inspired me. This time away would change me. I imagined myself: journal and fountain pen in hand, resting on the swing by the pond, writing eloquent prose as puffy white clouds drifted over a robin's egg blue sky.

"Now, let's repeat the introductions. Then I'll answer any questions you have."

I sipped my tea and nearly spit it back out. It was bitter and dark, with a mossy flavor.

"Wait till you try the coffee alternative." The man next to me whispered.

I glanced over. He smiled, his eyes a deep brown that matched his thick but neatly trimmed beard.

"Coffee alternative?"

"It's a caffeine-free establishment."

I groaned quietly and he nodded in response.

". . . and I'll start," Venetia said. "As you know, I'm Venetia Valentine and while we don't like using titles here, I suppose you'd call me the director of Idyll Weiss. It's a role I've been proud to fill for the past five years. I've been coming here for decades though. This place is magical." Her face softened and she motioned to the next person.

"I'm Paula Hayden," the woman who'd stuck the little coaster under my mug said. Her face resembled a bulldog, but her body looked more like a greyhound. She had medium-length gray-brown hair that was pinned back with two fuchsia clips on either side of her head. The girly barrettes were at odds with her masculine build, the flannel shirt buttoned up to her neck, and she wore baggy jeans. "I've taught MFA students creative writing at Princeton in a previous life," Paula smiled wryly. "Now, I'm the cook and chief bottle washer."

Polite chuckles sounded around the table.

Ruby introduced herself as the jill-of-all-trades, an award-winning poet, and the winner of a previous Ruth Lilly Poetry Prize. Now that we were all seated, and the lighting was better I could see her features more. Like the other instructors, Ruby was in her late sixties or early seventies. She was plump and dressed in an ill-fitting dress in a puke green shade. I wondered if she and Venetia shopped from the same catalog.

Next were the five of us writers.

"I'm Imani Williams," said a curvy woman with dark brown skin and a smoky voice. "I'm happily divorced, no kids, from Shelburne where I write poetry when I'm not working as a nurse."

"Thanks, Imani," Venetia offered her a small nod before moving to the woman next to her. She was young—maybe the youngest of all of us there—and as pale as moonlight. She also had the longest dreadlocks that I'd ever seen. They were dotted with beads, both colored and silver that sparkled in the light.

"Oh, um, hi." She gave an awkward wave. "I'm Gwen. Gwen Stevens. I write horror by night. By day I work in a youth rehab center. I'm from Hubbardton and my boyfriend and I live off the grid, so I'm used to rustic."

Everyone smiled back at her.

The guy to my right introduced himself as Liam Stone.

"I live in Bennington and write military history. My area of focus is on World War Two."

He didn't mention anything about his relationship status, and I found myself strangely disappointed by that.

Venetia's penetrating gaze landed on me.

"Hello," I felt as tongue-tied as I had the first day of middle school. "I'm Flora Rossi. I'm glad to be here." I forced a smile. "I write family drama. I have two books published by a small press and another that I'm halfway through. I live in Winooski and I'm single, so I have plenty of time to focus on my craft. But I've been blocked for the past few months, so this retreat came at just the right time."

First, I couldn't think of what to say, now I couldn't shut up.

Venetia nodded. "Welcome, Flora." She looked to the only

other man in the room sitting on my left. He was a little chubby and dressed like a banker.

"Hello everyone, I'm George Hartford. I'm the father of two kids under age four, so basically haven't slept in the past few years."

We chuckled.

"I write mysteries but haven't been published yet." He smoothed a hand over his goatee. "But I do have a couple of agents who've requested sample chapters recently, so that's exciting. Oh, and I live in Middlebury with my beautiful wife, Cynthia."

"Wonderful." Venetia pointed to the empty seat next to her. "You'll meet Randi Madison tomorrow morning. She's the last of our little band of leaders but she had to attend to a few things this evening. Randi is a ghostwriter and has written for some very well-known celebrities. Not that she can tell you who they are."

A sudden gust of wind rattled the mullioned windows.

"Due to the weather and the darkness, we'll save the grounds tour for tomorrow," Venetia motioned to the door, "But Ruby will show you where to find the kitchen, the common room, and your sleeping quarters, for those who haven't yet. And of course, she'll point out the ever-important outhouses."

I groaned inwardly. Going out in the rain to use the bathroom was not going to be my favorite part of this retreat. What was left of the floor space around the giant slab table was minimal, so we lined up single file and waited in awkward silence. Paula moved to the front of the line and led us out.

Last, in line, I glanced back to see Venetia staring after us with a look on her face I couldn't place. For some strange reason, I shivered.

Chapter Three

Even though the room was dark and cool and the sound of rain splatting against the window hypnotizing, I couldn't sleep. Images that I carefully packed away every day slipped out of their boxes and ran rampant in the darkness. A mosaic of pictures appeared on the back of my eyelids: the swirling strobe of blue lights, the sparkle of crushed glass on the pavement, and the dark stain of blood across my shirt and down my pants.

My breath had quickened in my chest. I couldn't afford a panic attack, not now. Forcing my breathing to slow, I focused on something tangible like my therapist, Monica, had taught me to do in these situations. My sheets were tangled around my legs like seaweed. Sheets. That was good. Safe. I took another slow breath.

What else about the sheets?

They were soft. Softer than I'd expected. It was a surprise how comfortable the bed was. I'd expected something more monastic—maybe a hard cot with a scratchy wool blanket. Instead, the bed had snuggly sheets and a cozy handmade quilt.

The air outside the bed was cold. The tip of my nose chilly as I burrowed deeper into the blankets. The little woodstove Ruby had pointed out when she'd shown me the room must be out. She'd said that only staff took care of the fires, the guests shouldn't touch them. Had she purposely not filled mine with enough wood for the night?

My heartbeat slowed a little more.

I focused on other aspects of the room around me. It was dark now, but as I closed my eyes, I tried to remember what I'd seen when I'd first walked in. Fresh flowers sat in a vase on the small, antique dresser. The vase was green, I was pretty sure. A rag rug lay over the painted wood floor and there was a beautiful canopy over the bed, made of what looked like hand-embroidered cotton.

My heartbeat was normal again. Relieved, I turned onto my side. The rain slowed and plonked on the window making smeary trails down its surface. But beyond the dark clouds, I could see the thinnest sliver of the moon. Tomorrow, I'd attend my first workshop. I could hardly wait to get the advice, tips, and tricks the leaders would share, especially Venetia.

Finally, my body grew heavy, my breath slow and regular. A sound played on the periphery of consciousness. A low moan. A cow? Someone in the room next door?

I could get up, find out what it was.

That was my last thought before sleep pulled me under.

***

The next morning dawned bright and crisp. All signs of last night's storm were gone. It was a quintessential Vermont autumn day. The sky was periwinkle, clouds stretched like gauze in patches. The sweet thick scent of smoke from a woodstove filled the air. I breathed deeply before throwing off the heavy quilt and stretching.

As I dressed, I inspected the room more closely. It showed a little wear. There were hairline cracks in the plaster walls and a few tiny moth holes in the canopy over the bed. Still, it was charming. An old-fashioned wash basin and pitcher sat on a stout wood table across the room. Next to it was a bar of soap, a wooden handled scrub brush, and a stiff-looking hand towel. I walked over to it. The mirror above the table showed a tired-looking thirty-something-year-old, her dark hair laced at the temples with gray. They'd sprouted in the weeks after the accident.

A knock sounded on my door and it swung open.

"Good morning." Ruby was bright-eyed. "Slept well I hope?" Her eyes scanned the room behind me. I changed my position in the door slightly, cutting off her line of sight. The woman had no sense of personal boundaries.

"Fine, thanks."

"Breakfast is ready. We give everyone a good morning wake-up call at six-thirty. But you must be an early bird, already up and dressed."

She went on without waiting for me to reply. "Breakfast is always served at seven and if you miss it, well." She shrugged her plump shoulders.

"I'll go hungry?"

She laughed, as though I'd said something funny. "See you downstairs. You remember the way?"

I nodded and closed the door as she moved off to the next room.

Ruby was right. I was naturally an early riser. Not on purpose though. Sleep hadn't been good for me in the past couple of years. I made my bed and tidied up before walking into the hallway and pulling the door closed. I was going to get into my writing groove here, I knew it.

Gwen passed as I turned to go down the stairs.

"Good morning."

She grunted and yawned in response. "Sorry. This is about three hours too early to be awake."

I laughed.

"You're not one of those chipper early risers who brags about the five hours of self-care they've done before normal people are even awake, are you?"

I held up my hand. "No, I promise."

"What do you write again?" She fiddled with one of her dreadlocks.

"Family drama. And you write horror, right?

She nodded and started down the stairs, which squeaked and squawked underfoot.

We were the last to arrive in the dining room, which I'd spied through the doorway while standing at the fireplace in the common area. It looked much different in the daylight. Gone were the gloomy shadows and darkened corners. Instead, pale sunlight fell in wide bars through the windows. Like the meeting room, we'd been in last night, the dining room had the same mullioned windows. The entire interior was wood, without a scrap of sheet rock in sight. But in place of the long, oversized table there were small round ones, just big enough for two scattered around the room. A narrow buffet stood along the wall opposite a small fireplace and was covered in steaming platters and napkin-lined baskets. The smells of buttery, delicious food filled the air. My stomach growled in response, and I fell in line behind Gwen.

"The only thing missing is the scent of coffee," I whispered to Gwen.

She groaned in response. "What is wrong with these people?"

"Everything here is fresh, homemade, and organic," Ruby smiled as she stocked a table with pottery plates. Thick mugs, silverware, and cloth napkins were nearby.

"It looks delicious," I said, and meant it. While Gwen passed over the scrambled eggs and bacon, murmuring "vegan," I helped myself. After adding a still-warm berry-studded muffin and some blueberries to my plate, I looked around the room for an empty seat. Gwen had scooted in next to Liam. There was only one spot at a table along the back wall. Weaving my way through the tables, I paused by the empty seat.

"Do you mind sharing?"

Imani looked up, seemingly startled. Her head had been bent over a book, but she shrugged and moved the book a little closer to her side of the table when I sat down.

I cleared my throat. "Is this your first writers' retreat?"

She didn't say anything for a moment, and I wondered if she was going to ignore me completely. Finally, she raised her head and glanced at me.

"No," she sipped from her mug. "But it's the first one I've attended in Vermont."

"Really?" I spread a thick smear of butter on my muffin.

"Mmm. I attend one a year—a conference or a retreat—but they've all been out of state." She glanced back at the book. It was a journal or maybe her writing notebook. It was the most exquisite one I'd ever seen. The pages were thick and creamy, the cover looked like it was covered in velvet or some similar luxurious fabric. Her handwriting was loopy and scrawling and slanted in neat rows across the page. In the margins she'd drawn little figures or doodles—

She snapped the book shut, the ribbon bookmark fluttering

free from its pages.

"I'm sorry. I wasn't trying to read it," I smiled and stirred my tea. "Just admiring your journal. It's beautiful."

The turquoise cover shone in her hands as she stood abruptly.

"Thanks," her voice was curt. She mumbled something about her room. My cheeks grew hot as she left me sitting alone. I glanced around surreptitiously to see if anyone else had noticed our exchange. George, leaning back in his chair at the table nearest me, gave a wink.

"She's not a morning person?"

"I guess not."

"You're welcome to join us." He nodded toward the table he shared with Ruby. Paula swept into the room and began refilling the plates and platters at the buffet line.

"We take turns," Ruby said as I scooted my chair close to their table. "I have lunch duty and Randi has dinner tonight. We try to work around our cycles."

"Cycles?" I speared a juicy strawberry. The food was amazing.

"You know early birds and night owls. Part of what makes this Retreat Center successful is that it allows for individuality of the staff. You won't usually see Venetia or me at breakfast. But today is a special day, the first we welcome our new attendees." She took a big bite of muffin. Some of the berries popped open in a red spurt on her lips.

"How long have you worked here?" George asked.

"Mmm," Ruby waved a hand as though it would hurry her chewing, then dabbed her lips with the cloth napkin and swallowed.

"I started coming to Idyll Weiss eighteen years ago. I've been living and working here for the past eleven." She took a sip of tea. I wondered if it was the same mossy-tasting stuff I'd had last night. "It doesn't seem possible it's been that long already."

"How long has the Retreat Center owned this space?" George-the-Chubby-Banker as I'd come to think of him, sipped a glass of orange juice.

"Oh, a long time. She was here before me." Ruby glanced at Venetia across the room, then back at George. "Even when she was at the height of her literary success, this was her hideout from the world." She giggled in a girlish way. It was kind of creepy.

"I'd love to ask you a few more questions about the history of Idyll Weiss," George said.

"We'll have lots of time to chat while you're here, George." Ruby flashed him a smile. She had dimples in her pink cheeks and her face transformed into a younger woman's when she smiled. "But right now, I'm needed in the chicken coop."

George sighed softly as she walked away.

"The book I'm working on is set at a Retreat Center. I plan to get a lot of research done this week. That's going to be hard to do though if I can't get my questions answered." He pushed his glasses up and glanced at me. "Sorry. I know it's not all about *me, me, me.* Though I do like the sound of that." He laughed.

"You said you were working on a mystery, right?"

He nodded.

"What's the subgenre?" I sipped my glass of juice. Unlike breakfast, it wasn't delicious, but overly sour.

"I write crime fiction—sort of like Louise Penny crossed with Lee Child. Do you read either of them?"

I shook my head.

"Your loss," he chuckled.

"I've forgotten what you write. I'm sorry." He drew his

eyebrows together and squinted at me. "Is it romance?"

I shook my head.

"Oh, wait! Family drama, right?"

"Yes."

"I've got enough of that in my everyday life. Between work and kids and the house—" He broke off and laughed at himself.

"Sorry. I love my life. It's just . . . a lot sometimes. That's why I'm so grateful I was chosen to attend."

I nodded. "Do you write in a series? That seems popular in that genre." I folded my napkin back up and laid it near my plate. The room buzzed with conversation. It felt cozy and warm. Again, a wave of satisfaction washed over me. This was going to be a good week.

"Yes," George put his silverware on his empty plate. "My amateur sleuth is a guy who's a lawyer in a coroner's office. It might sound like a weird place for a lawyer to work, but they do. Anyway, Claude, the main character, starts to wonder about some of the bodies brought in."

I nodded at the same time a bell clanged.

"That's the call to workshops, folks," Venetia said from across the room. "You'll hear that bell frequently in your time with us."

"You can just leave those there, Flora." Paula stood with her arms crossed and nodded at me. I'd stacked our empty plates and put the silverware on top. "I'll clear everything in a minute."

The bell clanged again, and I envisioned an old-fashioned school bell.

"Your first class begins!" Venetia said with a small smile.

"Does this remind anyone else of reform school?" Liam asked under his breath as we filed toward the meeting room.

"You were in reform school?" George asked loudly.

Everyone turned to look.

George grinned. "Just kidding."

The antler atrocity overhead wasn't as obvious in the day-light. It blended in with the wood-paneled ceiling above. The room was set up the way it had been last night. As I'd expected, the sunlight spilled in the windows. Imani was already sitting in the same seat from the night before, her head bent over the beautiful journal. At every place, there was a green folder, a notebook, and three freshly sharpened pencils. A wave of giddiness washed over me. It reminded me of the first day—the best day—of school growing up. Everything was fresh and new. All those possibilities waiting for you.

"We'll begin with an introductory session and that will lead into a free-writing time. We think you'll find these lectures the perfect way to spark ideas and get the muse to come out to play," Venetia explained. "Before we get started though—you'll remember what I mentioned last night about your laptops. We've provided you with notebooks which you're welcome to use." She waved a hand toward the table. "Or if you've brought your own, feel free to use them instead."

"Now, if everyone is ready, let's get started."

Chapter Four

"Sorry, I didn't realize this spot was taken," a man's voice said. I was lying on a bench swing by the pond, my arm over my eyes. I swung it aside. Liam stood nearby.

"Oh, no," I sat up. "Please sit."

The swing swayed gently under his weight.

"I was writing, I swear. I just got sleepy all of a sudden."

"Must have been the lumberjack lunch." Liam grinned. He had a very good smile. Flipping his notebook open, he rifled through several of the lined pages before finding where he'd left off.

"Have you written all that just now? I'm jealous."

"What? Oh, yeah." He glanced from the notebook to me and then back again. "Yeah. Well, it doesn't usually come so easily. You know how it goes."

I did know. Our assignment for the afternoon was to find something in nature and correlate it to our writing process.

My notebook was still blank but I nodded at Liam.

"There's something about this place—or maybe it's being away from regular life and everything I need to do—that's helping me. You?"

I laughed and shook my head. "Afraid I've been doing more relaxing than writing. But you're right, I think it was lunch.

I'm not used to eating so much in the middle of the day. The food is really, really good."

"Better than the beverages."

I laughed. Sunlight bounced off the pond's surface and made glittering flashes of light. Two ducks paddled silently along the shore, periodically diving down for food.

"This is a good spot we picked."

A little shiver went through me at the word *we*. I liked how it sounded coming out of Liam's mouth.

As though on cue, a fish jumped out of the water. When it fell back in, shiny beads of water cascaded into the flat surface of the pond's surface, and then slowly spread out into rings.

"What are you working on?" He turned to me.

His eyes were brown—really brown like that French hot chocolate I only ever drink when I visited Montreal. His gaze searched my face. Stupidly, I blushed like a teenager.

"Oh, um, it's a piece of poetry actually." I motioned to the notebook in my lap, its pages creased and crumpled where I'd pressed them against my chest during my nap.

"You're a poet."

I shook my head. "No, not really. Just trying to get out of my routine, try something new."

"I'm not a poet either." The megawatt smile came again. I felt my throat constrict a little, making it hard to breathe.

I hoped he wouldn't ask if I had an interest in history. I was a terrible liar. I fell asleep more than once in Professor Morey's History of Ancient Civilization course. Once, my classmate jabbed me because I was snoring so loudly.

"I'm going to move down over there." Liam pointed to an Adirondack chair on the far side of the pond. "I can't write around other people." His expression was apologetic. "No offense."

"Sure. Of course." I tried not to feel disappointed as he moved off toward the big weeping willow and the chair tucked under it.

Maybe I needed a change of scenery too. Somewhere away from the warm sun and the temptation to stare at Liam.

It was unseasonably warm. Maybe a walk would clear my head. I stood and gathered my notebook and pen, then pushed my way through some scraggly bushes, to a little sign that read, *Nature Path*.

It was quiet in the woods; the only sound was birds chattering overhead. As I walked, it struck me again how lucky I was to be here. How lucky each of us was. I'd overheard Ruby telling Imani the night before that there were more than three hundred applicants. Because the retreat only ran every three years and it was so small, the selection process was difficult. My eavesdropping had been cut off after that because George had started asking if anyone had an extra flashlight.

Nearby, a branch broke. I turned.

Gwen stepped out of the foliage onto another path that ran parallel to the one I was on. She had a dreadlock in her fingers which she rolled over and over. She wasn't holding a notebook. Maybe, like me, she was struggling to get into her groove. Or maybe she was in the brainstorming phase and liked to do it all mentally. I had a friend like that in college. She drove me nuts, never focusing on our conversations and asking me to repeat myself over and over. But when Gwen turned in my direction, her pale face looked pinched. She walked quickly and cast a furtive look over her shoulder.

That's when I noticed there was someone else on the path behind her. A shadowy shape, without form. Gwen too, seemed to feel it approach. Rather than glancing back casually though, she whirled around, her hippie skirt making a wide arch. Her face in profile looked alarmed, maybe even panicked. She moved slightly back and branches hid her face from view. I hunkered down between a sapling and a bush, waiting to see what would happen.

The figure stopped moving. The undergrowth and branches were too dense for me to make out any telling details from this angle—man or woman, tall or short—I couldn't tell. Someone spoke unintelligibly. The shadowy figure or Gwen? The birds nearby drowned out any stray words I might have collected. Gwen shifted slightly and I saw her face again. She shook her head, then put her hands over her ears briefly as though trying to drown out the person's words.

Then the shadow retreated, going back the way it had come. I expected Gwen to continue to the pond. Instead, she glanced over her shoulder, her eyes swept the small clearing. She looked upset, her eyes bright like she might be trying not to cry.

I was still wedged between a pine tree and an overgrown bush but raised my hand when she glanced toward me. Either she didn't see me or ignored me. She brushed the dreadlock back over her shoulder and darted down another path in a different direction.

Maybe I should go after her. Ask if she was all right. Or should I take the other path and follow the shadowy figure? Who was it and what did they want with Gwen?

I looked back from where I'd come. From the little knoll where I stood, I could see the side of the looming house and a handful of outbuildings. One was a barn, another two appeared to be sheds. Paths led from one building to the other and others led into the woods, but I couldn't tell where they went.

The bell sounded crisp and clear in the mid-afternoon air. At first, I wondered what it was for. Then remembered: we were supposed to share our work when we returned from this afternoon's writing. I cursed under my breath. I didn't have anything. Not a single sentence, only a lot of half-started ones that I'd scribbled out. I looked down at my notebook, willing my brain to think of something—anything—but was met with silence.

This retreat was a waste. You're too broken to write again, a little voice whispered. *You're ruining your only chance here.*

"Time for our next session," a woman's voice called out. A small, wispy-looking woman walked down the path where Gwen and the figure had stood moments before. Her eyes were cornflower blue, and her short hair was cut like Tinkerbell's.

I exited my hiding spot, smoothing down my clothes and pulling a twig free of my hair. Retracing my steps. I soon caught up to her. When she saw me, she stuck out her hand. Her grip was surprisingly strong.

"I'm Randi. And you must be Flora."

I nodded. "Nice to meet you. I, uh, didn't have much luck. With the writing assignment. Do you think I should still go to the session?"

Randi laughed, the sound like a string of jingle bells.

"Of course! You wouldn't be the first writer to be hit with writer's block here. Follow me and let me get you a mug of something delicious. Tea? Or perhaps hot cider?"

"Anything with caffeine?"

She laughed again and shook her head. "You won't find any of that here. But don't worry, if you're feeling sleepy, I have just the thing."

We started down the path and then I remembered Gwen.

"Gwen—she went that way," I pointed to the trail I'd seen her take.

"She'll find her way back. That bell can be heard for nearly a mile on a clear day like this. Now, tell me where are you from, Flora?"

***

I'd chosen a seat far away from the narrow windows, hoping that the lack of warm sun falling on me would keep me more alert. Still, I found myself blinking too many times in succession. I shifted in my seat and casually hid a yawn in my shoulder when a heavy, green clay mug appeared on the table nearby.

"Your elixir," Randi whispered, slipping away before I could thank her.

Ruby was instructing this afternoon. Her assignment had been to study an element of nature, capture its essence, and tie it into our current work-in-progress somehow. I wondered how the others had done.

Ruby looked around the room. Her gaze settled on Liam. "Would you like to share first?"

Liam nodded before clearing his throat and reciting a beautiful and complicated description of a butterfly he'd observed. He compared its lightness and tenacity with that of the military maneuvers of the *something-something brigade* during the Battle of Berlin . . .

I tuned out and sipped the tea. Unlike the horrible stuff Ruby had given me last night, this was slightly sweet. It had an earthy undertone but wasn't unpleasant. I drank most of the mug before realizing it. Within minutes my mind felt clearer and more focused. It reminded me of when I used to suck down a pot of coffee cramming for exams. I swallowed the last bit, wondering what was in it.

"And you, Flora?" Ruby's pink cheeks were pulled up in a smile, but to me, her eyes looked wary. Since the awkward exchange when I was sopping wet, I'd felt uncomfortable around her. And she still seemed miffed.

Squaring my shoulders, I pulled my notebook closer and pretended to read. Rather than halting prose, the words came like magic, spilling from my mind and out of my mouth easily. It was about the cycles of life I'd observed, the death of one thing meant the sustenance of something else, and how the connection breeds creativity. I circled back at the end, sharing how all this interconnectedness tied in with my current work-in-progress. How creativity, like connectivity, is much more than simply what we can see in the physical world.

When I stopped, the room was quiet. I glanced up. Ruby's smile was broad, Liam grinned at me, a flash of white between his dark beard. Imani looked like she'd just sucked on a lemon.

George sat back in his chair and gave a wolf whistle. "Nailed it."

My cheeks turn pink. Where had all that come from? I wished I'd have written down everything I said. I eyed the empty mug. What was in that stuff?

As I leaned back in my chair, I noticed Gwen's seat was still empty.

"Where's Gwen?"

"She had a headache and is lying down," Ruby said. "As before friends," she glanced at George, "let's save our feedback until the end of this mini-session. And now, on to you, Imani."

Chapter Five

By late afternoon the warm sunshine was gone and dark clouds lined the sky. Like bouncers, they blocked out the rays of the sun. I paced in the library—a beautiful, tiny circular room tucked into the center of the house—and admired the bookshelves. They were built on a curve, following the walls of the room, and stretched from floor to ceiling.

It smelled perfect: dry and dusty but with an undertone of lemon polish and the scent of old wood. Overhead, ancient-looking beams supported the creamy ceiling. A thick, medium-sized table filled the middle of the room, round like the walls. There were no windows and it seemed inevitable that one would feel claustrophobic. Instead, the space felt safe, like the blanket forts you made as a kid.

I wanted to dictate my writing into my phone, but it would use up the battery. Even though there was no signal, I kept it with me more out of habit than anything else. It had eighty-five percent left. Maybe it would be okay? I'd had such success during our morning session, I wanted to try again. I cleared my throat and opened the notes recorder app. I started to speak, working on a particularly challenging part of the manuscript I'd been sweating over for weeks.

I'd just moved into the dialogue—a painful conversation

between mother and daughter—when the library's door flew open. I jumped and whirled around. Gwen stood in the doorway, her shoulders shaking and breath coming in fast, hard gasps like she'd been running.

"Gwen?"

She glanced around the room, her eyes searching for something.

"What is it?"

Her face was even paler than usual and there was a long, red splotch across one cheek.

"Are you okay?" I moved toward her.

She glanced over her shoulder, then shut the door and crossed the space between us in a few steps. Grabbing my shoulders, her fingers bit into the flesh.

"I can't stay here." Her mouth was close to my ear, her breath tickling my skin. "They're crazy."

"Who?"

She jerked her head toward the door. "Th—"

The door opened again. This time it was Gwen who jumped and whirled toward it. Imani stood framed in the door, a loose tunic moving slightly over her curvy hips from the breeze the door had made. Gwen leaped away from me as though she'd touched an electric fence.

Imani looked annoyed. "Oh. I didn't realize this space was taken. I'll find somewhere else."

"No!" Gwen's voice was shrill in the small room. "We were just leaving."

"Were you?" Imani frowned.

"Yes," I grabbed my notebook and phone. "Gwen and I are . . . going for a walk. For inspiration."

"Oh." Imani drifted over to the thick table and lowered a

stack of books to its surface. She sat and flipped through the pages of the top book, apparently having already lost interest in us.

"See you at the next session."

Imani hummed a response.

Gwen walked so close to me that heat from her body pressed against my shoulder blades as we walked silently down the narrow hallway. There wasn't room here to talk, the narrow corridor pressed close on both sides. I hurried toward the front door, mind racing.

Gwen made a strangled squeaking sound as a figure descended the staircase. The area was shadowy, the single lantern at the top of the stairs not throwing enough light to fully illuminate it.

"Excuse me," Liam passed by, his white smile visible in the dim light. I smiled back stiffly. "Forgot my notebook." He headed down the hallway in the direction of the classroom. Gwen and I continued outside and stood on the front walkway.

The air had cooled off and goose bumps rose on my arms.

Gwen's clammy fingers wrapped around the back of my elbow. "Please," she whispered hoarsely. "I need to get away from here."

"Let's go for a walk, and you can tell me—"

"No. You don't understand." She took a deep breath, her voice an octave lower when she spoke again. "You have a car, don't you?"

"A car?"

"They picked us up at the bus station. I—I don't have any way to—to get away."

My mind struggled to keep up. It was clear she was upset. Something had happened. But why leave? We'd just gotten here. And even if I wanted to, I couldn't give her a ride to the nearest bus station. We were hours away.

"Gwen—"

"I need to go. Now," Gwen's voice shook a little at the last word. Her face was so white and her eyes so large they looked almost cartoonish. I glanced around. Beyond the little portico where we stood, the trees swayed in an increasingly strong wind. Dark clouds stuttered across what little sky could be seen over the treetops.

"I get it. You're upset. And I—"

"Please. I know you don't know me, but you've got to believe that this is life or death."

Clearly, Gwen was having some kind of mental health emergency. I was ill-suited to deal with it though. But I hesitated. It hadn't been that long ago that I'd been in the middle of my mental health crisis. The images I kept locked away in the box in my mind threatened to squeeze out, but I shoved them back in.

"I think you should talk with Venetia or one of the other instructors—"

"No!" She said it so forcefully that I stepped back instinctively. Her eyes filled with tears. "I don't want them to know I'm leaving. It's not . . . it's complicated." A single tear slipped out, glittering on the curve of her marble cheek for a second before disappearing.

A memory popped into place; a cousin much older than me who'd had some sort of mental health crisis. It had all been kept very hush-hush by my grandmother and aunts.

"Nervous breakdown," one had said in a loud whisper before realizing I'd entered the kitchen to get a snack. "Poor thing couldn't handle life anymore." My cousin had been admitted to the psych ward.

Was Gwen dealing with something like that? If so, she needed help, not a ride.

"All right." I forced my voice to be soothing even though my mind continued to race.

Her shoulders sagged and she pressed her lips shut hard over her teeth as though to stop herself from saying anything else. She looked younger than ever. Her thin, fragile hands strayed to her dreads and tugged on the ends.

"All right," I repeated. "What about your things?"

"I don't need anything. I grabbed this before I found you." Gwen pulled a brightly embroidered clutch from her wide hippie skirt. "I have my ID and money and everything. Please. Can we go? I'll—I'll pay you for the gas and your time. Whatever. Just please."

She looked like a lost fairy in the pages of *Grimm's Fairy Tales*. I swallowed hard. I had to do what was best for her, not what necessarily felt right. I wanted to help her. But doing what she asked seemed irresponsible to me, reckless even. If she were having a mental health crisis, taking her away from here wasn't a safe option.

"I need to go back and get my purse. My keys are in it."

She started to shake, like one of the trees nearby. First her arms, then her torso and head which she shook vigorously from side to side.

"No. Don't go back there."

"Gwen, what are you talking about?" I intentionally kept my voice soft and neutral but could hear the frustration in it. "What happened?"

"I can't . . ." She sighed half-exasperation, half irritation. "I'll tell you. But once we're in the car, away from here."

"Okay," I said slowly. "But to do that, I need to get my keys. Do you want to come with me or go to my car? It's that way." I pointed to the little path that led to the makeshift parking area.

Gwen glanced around, eyes furtive. Drugs? Could that be it? Maybe she was having a bad trip.

"I'll go to your car." Her voice was barely more than a whisper. "I can't stay here. I'm too exposed."

"All right. It will just take a minute."

"Hurry."

I nodded and walked quickly back into the house.

Ruby was standing near the doorway, the big, brass bell in hand.

"Perfect timing." Her smile made her pink cheeks bunch up like a chipmunk's. "I was just about to notify everyone that the next session is starting. I saw you and Gwen out here a few minutes ago. She looked a little upset. Is everything okay?"

"Yes, fine. Good," I said. Then, "Do you know where Randi is?" I still didn't trust Ruby.

Two matching rows of creases appeared on Ruby's forehead and her smile faltered.

"Randi? In the kitchen I believe, doing dinner prep."

"Great, thank you."

"Is there something I can help you with?" Ruby readjusted her stance, partially blocking my way into the building.

"No, thanks." I maneuvered past her, hopefully without making it obvious that I wanted to get away. "I just had a quick question for her."

Strains of "Bobbie McGee" wafted down the hallway. I followed it to the kitchen and pushed the door open. How in the world was there a radio playing? Randi had her back to the door, hunched over a big, copper sink. She was wrestling with some sort of vegetation in it.

". . . call you my lover, call you my friend—" Her voice was an off-key warble.

"Randi?"

She straightened, cranked the water off, and turned around, hands dripping.

"Oh, hi. Sorry about that," Randi wiped her hands on the towel she wore around her waist like an apron. "I didn't hear you come in."

She moved to the sideboard and turned the knob down on a small radio. My eyebrows rose and she answered my unasked question. "It's solar-powered," she smiled.

I thought of Gwen waiting by my car, nervously eyeing her surroundings.

"I need your help. Something is going on with Gwen."

Chapter Six

Gwen was gone.

I'd waited for Randi to use the bathroom *"Old woman issue,"* she'd said, promising to hurry.

Minutes later, we'd shoved branches out of the way close to the parking area. It was deserted other than my car parked forlornly near a bush.

"Gwen," I called. A bird flapped out of a tree nearby.

"Gwen?" Randi called. "Yoo-hoo, Gwen. Where are you?" Randi surveyed the woods around us, pushing back wet branches to see through the dense undergrowth.

The ground around my car was still thick with mud and the doors were closed, windows up. I glanced inside as I skirted the car, but Gwen wasn't hiding in the backseat or crouched on the floor.

I swiveled, scanned the whole clearing but saw only the dense foliage and the tightly packed trees of the forest around me. We stood there for several long minutes. The sound of the tree branches clacking together and the scampering of little animals moving in the leaves gathering nuts and whatever else they stored. Far off, a bird let out a long, mournful call.

"Gwen," I called again. "Please, don't be mad that I brought Randi. She's here to help. We both are."

"Maybe she changed her mind and headed back to the Center," Randi said.

Gwen had been upset. The silent tears and look of fear were obvious. The jarring clang of the big, brass bell sounded for the second time from back at the house. Ruby liked to give a "gentle reminder" which was just a tardy warning in disguise.

I shrugged. "Maybe."

Had Gwen headed to town on foot? Or was she hiding in the woods right now, watching us? An uneasy curl of dread unfurled in my belly.

"I'll walk down the road. Maybe I'll see some signs of her," Randi offered. "Why don't you head back? You don't want to miss the next session. It's a good one."

"Are you sure?" I asked more out of politeness than a real desire to stay. Randi was probably right. We'd be out here looking for Gwen while she was probably back at the Retreat Center.

"Sure, I haven't gotten my walk in today anyway. I'll let you know if I find her, okay?" She smiled, her blue eyes crinkling at the corners.

"Thanks. I appreciate it."

She waved over her shoulder and headed further down the little path.

I circled my car one last time and turned, ready to head back to the house. The mud was squishy underfoot and sucked at my shoes. I'd just passed the passenger side door when something caught my eye. A small glitter of light in the mud near the front passenger tire. I stooped and picked it up. It was a bead, long and tubular, shiny silver with engraved markings all over it. Rubbing the mud away, I bit my lip.

It was one that Gwen wore in her dreadlocks. The pale snarls of her hair had been dotted with colorful beads and a handful of these shiny silver ones.

"Gwen?" I called one more time.

But only the whisper of the wind blowing through the jagged branches answered.

Chapter Seven

Someone had been in my room. I'd hurried back to the house to change shoes and put away the bead I'd found. I didn't know why but it seemed important that I keep it. As soon as I opened the door, I could tell something was off. Instead of the scattering of ponytail holders and bobby pins in a general heap on the bureau, they were stacked neatly. And where a jacket had been slung cockeyed over a hardback chair by the small table, it was now smoothed straight over the chair's back.

I stood in the middle of the room. Why would anyone come in here? Had they been looking for something? I hurried to the bureau and pulled open the top drawer. The old dresser gave a little squawk as I lifted my purse free. I looked through it. Everything was there—wallet, credit cards, cash. My fingers fumbled with the interior pocket. No keys. I must have shoved them in my jacket pocket when I arrived. It had been raining hard. I reached for the jacket on the back of the chair but there was nothing except a gas receipt in either pocket.

A little panicky feeling nipped at me, but I pushed it away. They had to be here somewhere. Wait. I'd had on my rain jacket when I got here. It was still hanging in the entryway.

Footsteps sounded in the hallway. There was a knock on the door and Venetia poked her head in. "Will you be joining us, Flora?" Her voice was friendly and warm, but she looked pointedly at her watch. I glanced at her distractedly and then nodded.

"Yes, of course. I was just—" I motioned around the room halfheartedly. I debated for a half second then said, "Someone was in my room."

Venetia's smile dimmed and she stepped into the space. It felt suddenly too small with both of us in there. Venetia was a tall woman. But now I felt dwarfed, like her kid sister.

"That's perplexing." She glanced around the room, nodded to the purse in my hands. "Is anything missing?"

I shook my head. "Just my keys."

"Your keys? And you're sure they were here?"

What if they were in my rain jacket? I glanced at the bureau again. My suitcase was shoved under the bed, and I hadn't looked there yet, or through the rest of my clothes. They could have ended up in one of the other drawers, mixed in with some clothes while I'd unpacked.

"No, I'm not sure. I'll look again later."

"You do that, and I'll make an announcement at lunch, shall I? Ask if anyone has seen them. That is if you don't find them in the meantime." Venetia looked like she was going to ask a question but shook her head and smiled at me again faintly.

"Maybe it was the fairies. We've had loads of things moved over the years, always showing up in the most unusual places," she chuckled. "Once, a participant lost her nightgown. It just poof," she exploded her fingers outward. "Disappeared. And then it appeared on a fencepost the next morning." Venetia laughed again. "Of course, that particular instance was the work of a comedy writer at the retreat."

I smiled but it was forced. "Have you ever thought of putting locks on the doors?" I asked as we moved from the room.

"No, never. This house is left in as natural a state as possible. No," she sighed through her nose. "It's much more of a bother than it's worth. We'd have to have master keys. And people would forget to leave them when they went home . . . it would cause more problems than anything. Do you see?"

I nodded but wasn't sure I did. I balked by the door, retraced my steps, and grabbed my purse before shutting the door behind me. Now that someone had been in there, I didn't feel safe leaving it in my bureau.

"Now, tell me. What do you think of our little bit of paradise so far?" Venetia led the way as we navigated the narrow hallway.

"It's wonderful," I said, and meant it. I pushed away the thoughts of Gwen and my keys and focused on the benefits of the Retreat Center. "I already feel inspired. I'm sure I'll have a breakthrough before I leave. The surroundings are beautiful, and the food is incredible. And the workshops have been excellent."

"I'm glad to hear it. This next session is one you'll enjoy." Venetia paused at the bottom of the stairs and turned to face me. "It's about tempting out our inner muse and what to do when she's being elusive. Paula teaches it and it is delightful. One of the best sessions in my opinion. Other than my own of course." She smiled. "And I believe we're scheduled for a one-on-one session tomorrow morning."

A thrill surged through my chest. I'd been hoping our individual session would be soon. Talking with Venetia casually was one thing. Being able to ask her opinions on my work, and maybe even be referred to some of her connections was another. Lost in a daydream of a book tour, I suddenly realized I was at the door outside the meeting room. I turned to say goodbye to Venetia.

"Oh, I almost forgot. I believe this is yours." Venetia pulled my notebook and pen from a bag I hadn't noticed her carrying. "You don't want to lose all your hard work."

Her fingers were warm as they connected with mine on the notebook. I blushed, wondering if she'd looked inside and seen my work. Or lack of it.

"Where'd you find it?"

"You left it in the hall. I'll see you later," she smiled again. The floorboards groaned softly under her feet as she moved back down the hallway.

What was wrong with me? Why was I losing everything?

I clutched the notebook and hurried to the session, which, as Venetia had predicted was already in progress. I slid into one of two open seats and glanced around. Liam was to my left and gave me a distracted half-smile. Imani ignored me and George sat back in his chair, tapping a pen against his chin. Gwen's chair was empty. I felt a little bubble of worry in my stomach but purposefully ignored it. Randi had probably found her out on the road, and they were on their way back.

". . . and so, when you get to those parts in your work-in-progress, what happens?" She looked around the table expectantly.

"You're more likely to procrastinate," Imani said. "Because everything starts to feel overwhelming."

Paula nodded. "Good, good. Yes. Procrastination is the death knell of many a fine story. What else?"

As the responses came from around the table, I doodled in my notebook without really seeing what I scribbled.

"What do you think, Flora?"

I glanced up; Paula's gaze was sharp on her hangdog face.

"Probably meandering thoughts and distractions." I folded my hands over my notebook. "It's easy to get caught up in everything out there and forget the importance of focus."

Paula nodded again. "True. So, you've all shared some very valid, important points. Writing isn't an easy task, though most non-writers tend to think that words fly effortlessly. That stories are crafted overnight. Now, let's look at a classic example of this struggle in early literature: James Joyce."

Paula's workshop probably would have been great if I could focus. But thoughts were pinging fast and hard in all directions. Had I made a mistake telling Randi about Gwen? Where were my keys? Had Venetia read my journal?

". . . so let's have George with Flora and Imani paired with Liam."

I jerked back to the present, feeling confused.

"Any questions?" Paula was already edging toward the door. "If not, I have some paperwork to look over. We'll meet back here in a half hour."

"Where's Gwen?" George asked.

Paula stopped and turned to face us. "Gwen had a family emergency. She's on her way back home. Now, please." Paula motioned for us to begin and left the room.

My stomach lurched. *Poor Gwen.* Maybe a death in the family. Or a sudden illness. I chewed the inside of my cheek. She must have been grief-stricken. But why come to me and not one of the retreat leaders? And she hadn't seemed wracked with worry, as much as frightened.

Liam shifted in his seat and frowned. "That's too bad," he said to the group at large. "It was hard enough to get in here. It's bad luck that she had to leave so soon and miss it." He gathered his notebook and other supplies and moved to a chair near Imani.

"What do you think happened to her?" George asked in a loud whisper.

Behind him, Imani wrote furiously in her journal, ignoring us.

"I . . . I don't know." Should I tell them what had happened? I hesitated.

"She seemed upset and asked me to give her a ride. I thought—"

"Wait, when was this?" George asked.

"Just a little while ago. Before class."

Liam cleared his throat. "Maybe we should save this for lunch. Our assignment—"

"I agree." Imani snapped her journal closed. "I don't want to waste time listening to a bunch of gossip."

"We're just worried about her, Imani." My voice was sharper than I'd intended.

"Family emergencies happen. I'm here to work on my writing," she emphasized the last word. "And after what we all went through to get here." She looked at each of us pointedly, "I would think you would be focused on that too."

Paula re-entered the room, saw us all talking, and frowned. "Working hard?"

"Absolutely." George flashed her a big smile. "We were just comparing notes. Paula, would it be possible for me and Flora to work somewhere else? Maybe out in the dining room?"

"That would be fine. All of you," she looked around the room, "feel free to move."

We'd barely made it out of the room before George asked again in a loud whisper, "So, what happened with Gwen? She asked you for a ride?"

I nodded. "She seemed desperate to get away."

"Well, that makes sense. I mean if something happened back home—"

"But she never mentioned it. Just asked me to help get her out of here. She didn't say anything about her family. She seemed more scared. Like someone was after her."

George shook his head. He'd taken the lead through the hallway and didn't respond until we'd entered the empty dining room.

"She didn't want to talk to Venetia or the others either," I added.

"Hmm, that's weird. You know her well?" His eyes were warm, a frown marring his otherwise smooth forehead.

"No. But she seemed, really, I don't know . . . unnerved. Randi was—maybe still is—out there looking for her. She said she'd walk down to the main road to see if she could find her."

George narrowed his eyes. "You think Gwen went to hitch a ride?"

"I have no idea," I said. "She didn't mention anything to you?"

He shook his head. "No. I've barely talked to her, other than discovering we're both originally from Rhode Island. Did you? Talk to her much?"

"No." A little bubble of guilt formed in my chest. "But I wish I had."

George leaned closer and whispered loudly, "We should search the property. See if we can find her or dig up anything else about this place. It's a little weird here."

"What? Weird how?" My hands stilled, notebook mid-flip.

"I don't know. Just a feeling I got when we arrived. Like something bad happened here. I'd love to know more about this house's history." George eyed the beams overhead. "We should check it out tonight after dark, so no one knows what we're doing. It'll be an adventure. Like we're the Hardy Boys."

"I don't think so." I wondered if his wife sometimes felt like she had three kids.

"Well, let me know if you change your mind. You know, if you're not too chicken." George bumped shoulders with me, then opened his notebook with a chuckle.

As we worked, I couldn't stop thinking about what he'd said. It wouldn't hurt to look around the grounds. On the other hand, maybe Imani was right. People had family emergencies. And what could we expect to find? I'd let it go, I decided.

But as George read back through the writing sample he'd worked on; I couldn't block out the images of Gwen's terrified face. The whiteness of her skin, the haunted, hunted look in her eyes.

"All right," I said. We'd just finished our assignment and were closing our notebooks. "Let's go and take a look around tonight."

Chapter Eight

"This is going to be fun, "George's voice was low but filled with excitement. We stood by the front door. I flicked my flashlight on.

"Yeah, just great." My tone was sour. It had started to rain, and the sound driving against the boards of the house and off the tin roofs over our heads was loud. At least it would hide the sound of us leaving.

"Cynthia will be proud of me. She's the braver of us, I'm more the brawn." He chuckled.

I was beginning to appreciate Cynthia the more I heard about her. George was proud of his family. He'd had Randi and me nearly in tears at lunch, telling us about his kids' antics.

"Dot told the pastor's wife during the children's sermon that her mommy and daddy liked to wrestle like Jacob and his brother Esau," he'd said, chortling. "The whole church was dead silent. I could feel Cynthia melting in embarrassment next to me. I was trying so hard to keep from laughing that I farted."

Randi had guffawed.

"It wasn't our best Sunday." George ate the final spoonful of yogurt. "Cynthia is wound pretty tightly. I'm way more laid back. We're complete opposites." He'd smiled into his yogurt.

"But it works for us, you know?"

I didn't know. My last long-term relationship had ended years ago, and I'd been too busy with work and taking care of my grandmother to bother trying to find someone after Jason and I split.

Nona had chided me, often trying to connect me with a bingo partner's grandson or one of her golfing caddies. It had been alternately humiliating and humorous. I missed it. I missed a lot of things about Nona. She'd been both mother and father to me.

I cleared my throat now and refocused on the task at hand.

The rain came down in streams and George and I were both drenched before we made it down the front steps. George wore a dark, high-end rain jacket which he'd said could withstand monsoons. My rain jacket only went to my thighs. I hadn't found my keys in either pocket. Worry nipped at my gut but I purposely ignored it. Right now, we were stupidly getting drenched looking for someone who very likely was across the state by now.

"Let's try the outbuildings first." George's voice was barely audible over the driving rain. Wind rattled the tree branches together and moaned around the eaves of the house. How long could someone be out in this kind of weather before hypothermia set in? Hopefully, we wouldn't find out.

The property had three outbuildings that I'd seen and several winding paths. Some of those trailed off into the woods, others to gardens or "quiet places" where we'd been encouraged to work. We walked toward the right of the Center, and a warren of trails.

I followed George to the closest outbuilding, a big two-story horse barn. The door had an oversized, old-fashioned latch, a big board dropped into two wrought iron u-shaped pieces of metal. We lifted the wooden plank away and stepped inside and shone our flashlights around.

It was dusty and dry. Huge spiderwebs hung in the corners, draping the wooden posts. A layer of hay covered most of the floor which looked like it could disintegrate under our feet. There were no animals.

I sneezed twice in succession, but it could barely be heard over the rain pounding on the tin roof overhead. Other than the cobwebs and hay, there wasn't much else in there. Some old, rusted machinery that had seen better days, a stained mattress against one wall and across the room, a ladder that was built of boards and climbed into a rectangular space above.

"Gwen?" I whispered loudly. "Are you here?"

"Yoo-hoo!" George yelled out at top volume. "Anyone in here?"

His voice startled me, and I half laughed, half gasped. The words bounced around the emptiness like a microphone in a large auditorium.

"So much for subtlety."

George snickered, pointing to the ladder. "Are we going up?"

I hesitated, then nodded.

"You first."

"Why me?"

"Cause I'll be here to gallantly catch you if you fall."

I snorted but started climbing up. The boards were rough under my hands and the sharp edges bit into my palms. I put my flashlight between my teeth and aimed it directly overhead. This made climbing even more awkward, but I didn't want to come face-to-face with a spider, or worse, a wild animal in the darkness.

The ladder was tall—taller than I'd first thought—and it felt like I'd been climbing forever when my head finally poked up into the open space of the second floor. The rain must be slowing down. It was quieter now, gentle drumming on the roof. I shone my flashlight around. The hayloft was stacked with tired, saggy bales. Some had split, their insides once tightly compacted, now loose. They reminded me of stuffed animals that had been ripped open.

"See anything?" George called up.

"Nope."

"Well, let's try the next building then. I'm getting cold."

"Already?" I asked, though my teeth had started to chatter.

I turned awkwardly and angled my flashlight downward. Placing my foot carefully on the rung below me, I paused.

What was that? A noise, a sort of mewling sound had come from the hayloft to my far left.

I swung the beam of light in that direction. The straw shook for a second and then stopped when the light hit it.

"Gwen? Is that you?"

Nothing.

"Gwen?" Louder this time.

Still nothing.

"I'll be right down," I told George who had started stomping his feet. He groaned as I swung my legs up and over the ladder. The floor fluctuated under my feet, swaying. Would it hold? An image of me falling through a weak spot on the floor came to mind. I shook it away.

The sound came again, so soft it was barely audible from behind the stack of hay. I stopped moving so I could listen, but the sound stopped at the same time my feet did. I was within a few feet now, the light from my flashlight moving erratically over the bales and floor and shadowy corners of the space.

I put my hands out in front of me, steadying the light, and swallowed. My throat was dry, my lips felt stuck together.

"Gwen?" It came out as a whisper.

The crying sounded again. I pinpointed its location. Moving around the hay bales in my path, imagining Gwen sobbing in the straw—

"See anything?" George's voice sounded very far away.

I crept around the side of the bales.

The space was empty.

Wait. What was that? Something orange and white. A hat? Someone's shirt, maybe. I bent down, then moved toward it in a crab walk, keeping the flashlight beam trained on the spot.

Bright eyes peeked up and a skinny cat launched itself at my hand. It gave a fake-sounding snarl but its claws bit into my skin. I yelped and fell backward. The cat seemed to glare at me, then bounded away, jumping over the hay bales in three quick leaps.

"Are you okay?" George called. "What happened? Are you dead?" He laughed.

My heart thundered in my chest; my breath came in too fast, hitching gulps.

Just a cat.

I forced myself to slow my breathing and clutched my hand to my chest. "No, I'm fine."

I tried to laugh too as I descended the ladder, but the throbbing in my hand made me wince. George noticed it as soon as I was back on the ground.

"You're bleeding. What happened?" He inspected it, then pulled an old-fashioned handkerchief from his pocket, neatly made into a square, and pressed it against my hand.

"I met a cat. I think it was feral."

A wave of tiredness washed over me unexpectedly. What were we doing out here? Gwen was probably ensconced in a hospital somewhere with her family, sitting by the bedside of her loved one while we were drenched, cold, and looking for clues for nothing.

"I can check the other buildings on my own." George seemed to read my emotions.

I shook my head. "I'll go with you."

"You sure your hand's okay?"

"Yeah, it's fine." Truthfully, the skin felt hot and burned. Stupid cat. It probably had some disease.

Chapter Nine

We walked to the next building, a shed, but a big, rusted padlock sat on the latch like a fat toad. A small sign in a curly script read, "private."

"Got any hairpins on you, Nancy?" George asked loudly above the wind.

"Nancy?"

"Drew." He grinned. His glasses were studded with tiny raindrops that sparkled like diamonds in the beam of my flashlight.

I shook my head. "Sorry."

He unwrapped something in silver foil and popped it in his mouth. "Chocolate. For courage. Want one?" He pulled a handful of mini chocolate bars from his pocket. "Sorry, they're a little squishy."

I shook my head. "Let's finish checking."

"I started carrying these when the kids were little. Well, littler. Then I got addicted. Sometimes it's the only thing that gets you through the library's story hour or another mindless playdate."

"Do you stay home with your kids?" I asked as we tromped through the undergrowth to the third building, a little further from the house.

George nodded. "I work part-time and have the kids home with me the rest of the time. My wife's an attorney, so it made more sense for her to work than me. I'm a loan officer at a bank."

"Ha. I knew you worked at a bank."

George looked at me with surprise. "How could you tell? Do I have that loan officer smell?"

I grinned as we followed a small, barely visible path tangled with undergrowth that hid most of the dirt trail. We pushed through branches that snagged our clothes and hoods.

The path ran out near the building. Weeds had grown up tall around what looked like a smaller version of the barn. We circled the building painstakingly slowly. A tumult of branches and rough undergrowth made it hard to move. It was a small building to have two doors. The weeds were trampled down by one of them. George pointed to it and I nodded, following him closer.

When he opened it, the smell of ammonia and the dry scent of hay hit us. I shone my flashlight around. Little boxes lined the walls. Clucks and murmurs followed my flashlight beam and I pulled back out of the building.

"Chicken coop." I covered my nose and mouth, bumping into George who was standing too close behind me.

"Disgusting creatures."

"That's it." I paused in the overhang of the coop to get out of the now-gentle rain. "There aren't any other buildings."

"What about that?" George pointed to yet another overgrown path that meandered drunkenly off the main drive.

Everything in me wanted to tell George to go ahead and explore it himself. My feet were wet and freezing. My hands felt blue with the cold and my nose had started to drip. But

I couldn't. I was worried about Gwen. Too worried? I knew what my therapist would say. That I was trying to be the hero for Gwen that I hadn't been able to be for Nona.

I shook the thought away.

"Fine." I motioned for him to follow me. "Last one."

Our flashlights bounced over a path so thick with tangled branches and thorn bushes that I almost gave up after about fifty steps. But George, as though sensing my reluctance, pushed me on.

"Just a little further. We'll turn around soon if we don't see anything."

And then, as if his words had conjured it, a small white building appeared ahead. The paint was chipped and peeling, but the boards were straight and the corners true. Its door—thick and wide—was rotting along the bottom edge. It was small—too small to be a house—but why would anyone build a shed this far from the other buildings?

"Do you know what that is?" George's voice was excited.

"I have no idea."

"It's an icehouse!"

"Oh."

"I've been researching these for the book I'm writing. They were what provided early Americans with refrigeration. Did you know—"

"Look." I grabbed his arm.

A band of yellow light flickered across the bottom of the door. I thought it was caused by my flashlight at first. But then I realized my flashlight beam was pointed at the ground.

"I need more chocolate," George breathed.

I ignored his response and walked hesitantly toward the old building. Like the first one, a small sign in curly writing warned that the building was private.

"We need a plan," my voice was hoarse.

"There aren't any windows," George mused. He extracted two chocolates from his pocket and popped them in his mouth in quick succession. "At least, there aren't any windows on either of these sides. Typically ice houses wouldn't have any but they could have been added later. If they used the building for something else.

"Let's check the other sides first. You go that way and I'll go this way. We'll meet around the back of the building."

I hesitated, then nodded.

Creeping closer to the building, I put my feet down carefully to avoid making noise, alerting anyone inside to my presence. I strained to hear something, anything, but couldn't. The rain had picked up again, slashing against the old clapboard and running in rivulets down my face.

Keeping one hand on the building for support, I made my way through the thigh-high tangle of brush. The foliage was shiny in the bright beam. There was no window on this side, and I was relieved when I rounded the corner. I'd made it to the back unscathed.

George appeared seconds later at the back side of the building.

"You were right about the windows." I motioned overhead. The building's blank wall faced the woods beyond.

"Did you hear anything?"

"Besides my heart racing a hundred miles a minute?" I tried for a smile, but guessed I looked uneasy. "No."

"Let's go back to the front."

Stumbling through the wet grass and undergrowth again, we got to the front of the building. The light under the door bounced and swayed slightly. George pointed at it, then mimicked putting our ears to the door itself. He reached it first and tentatively put his head to it. I followed.

At first, I didn't hear anything. Then a low hum started. Machinery maybe—and then silence. Then the humming began again. No, not machinery. It was voices. Singing? Chanting? The sound broke off again and the air felt suddenly empty in its place. The rain had slackened and over it, a single voice rose. It mumbled something quietly at first but then grew louder and louder. Still, the thick, old door muffled the words too much for us to make any of them out.

George pulled on my sleeve. He motioned me back toward a group of small pine trees nearby. I followed him.

"What is that?" His voice sounded excited, and his warm breath tickled the lobe of my ear.

"I don't know," I said. "But maybe—"

Boards groaned. Then something metallic scraped against something else. We crouched instinctively, watching the doorway. The ribbon of yellow light grew dimmer and dimmer. Then finally it went out.

The door creaked open.

A hooded figure stood framed in the doorway.

Chapter Ten

It was impossible to see who it was. The hood was drawn low over the person's head. A second figure followed, then a third, and then a fourth. There was a moment of silence as they stood in a single-file line. Waiting.

For what?

Finally, another figure came out of the door. It hesitated on the step before reaching back and pulling the door stiffly closed. This one wore a white robe that seemed to glow in the darkness around us. It was unnerving how silent the ghostly forms were. Without conversation, the first person began walking back toward the other buildings. The others followed.

I looked at George. When our eyes connected, I jerked my head toward the group and mouthed, "Follow them?"

He nodded, eyes wide behind his glasses.

Despite the fear of being seen, a pleasurable spike of adrenaline coursed through my body. I slipped from between the bunch of trees. As I passed, the pine needles released their fragrant Christmas-y scent. It felt strangely out of place here in this dark, gloomy place. George was right behind me, close enough that I could grab his arm if I needed to. The thought was oddly comforting.

The rain had stopped but water still dripped off the leaves

overhead. Clumps of dark clouds scudded across the sky though a small bit of moon peeked through. I could barely make out the white robe in front of us. Undergrowth grabbed at my legs and branches poked and jabbed. We moved as quietly as possible through the trees. A thick carpet of dead, wet leaves underfoot muffled our footsteps but was wet and slippery.

A branch under my foot cracked like a gunshot. I gasped instinctively, throwing a hand over my mouth.

George hauled me backward and down into a crouch, nearly pulling me off my feet.

"What was that?" a voice ahead called. The line had stopped moving.

"Shh," another answered. "It was nothing. An animal. Deer maybe."

I recognized both voices. The first was Ruby's. The second was Venetia's.

The group remained motionless. My heart ricocheted in my chest. It was so loud I couldn't believe they didn't hear it.

George exhaled softly when they started walking again.

"What were they doing?" His chocolate-scented breath was too close to my face. I shivered and stood up slowly. He followed.

"I don't know," I replied. "But we need to find out."

We watched the little group retreat to the house. Rather than go in the front door though, they veered around the side and stopped. Before entering the building by the kitchen entrance, they removed the dark cloaks. I was right: Venetia and Ruby were the two in front, followed by Randi and Paula. The figure in white paused. Someone in the group murmured something unintelligible.

Randi asked the white-robed figure something else or repeated her previous question. The person nodded once again and then turned to the kitchen door. Venetia held it open while the figure passed through, then raised her eyebrows at the group of women. Randi nodded slowly, followed by Paula and Ruby last. The shadows distorted her face and made her look ghoulish.

I shivered.

"I'm not sure weird is a strong enough word to describe that." George made a sound that was half laugh, half groan. He stuck his hand into his pocket but drew it out empty.

I shook my head. I felt dull and stupid like my body couldn't cooperate with my fuzzy brain. None of it made sense. The staff in that old building were in robes. And who was wearing the white one? My brain scrambled for a reasonable explanation. A theater production? Political statement? Druids? I shook my head again and looked at George.

"We should go back to the icehouse. We might find answers there."

George shook his head. "That's a bad idea. What if they check in on everyone? Maybe that's why they don't put locks on the doors. So, they can creep around and go into our rooms at night."

The idea made new goosebumps stand up on my arms. This time they weren't from the cold.

Everything in me wanted to return to my room, shed my wet clothes, and climb into bed. But we weren't going to find answers that way. I didn't know why this was so important to me, but I knew I couldn't rest, couldn't sleep until I figured out what was in that icehouse.

"I'm going," I stood up. My legs ached from crouching and

prickles ran up and down them.

"Are you sure?" George raised his eyebrows.

I nodded.

"I feel like a jerk letting you go alone."

"I'll be fine, George. They're all inside now. I'm just going to take a quick look and go straight back to my room."

He hesitated, then nodded. "Tell me what you find. I wish I had some chocolate courage to offer you, but I ate it all."

"I'll be fine," I repeated, wishing I believed the words. A sense of dread washed over me. I hadn't thought George would bow out and wished he'd insist on coming along.

"Be careful," he mouthed and backed away out of the underbrush and back toward the house. Every window was black like dead eyes staring out at me.

I shivered but forced my shoulders to straighten. It was just an old, empty building. Besides, whatever was in it might shed some light on what was going on. If nothing else, maybe it would give me some writing inspiration.

An animal of some kind moved in the undergrowth to my right, a cue for me to get moving. Following the muddy path back to the icehouse, I looked for clues but didn't see anything other than trampled grass and muddy footprints. The path to the small building seemed much shorter and I was soon at the door. I pulled the handle, but the door wouldn't budge. It had creaked and groaned when the others had left it, so it probably wasn't used often. Planting my feet on the top of two rickety steps, I pulled harder.

Nothing.

Just as I was about to let go and try for a better grip, a crack appeared. I yanked again, this time keeping my body closer to the door, using it as leverage. The gap widened. When it was large enough for me to squeeze through, I shouldered my way in.

Chapter Eleven

It was very dim inside, too hard to see anything other than hulking black and dark gray shapes. The only light came from the doorway, but it was watery and useless. I grabbed my flashlight, grateful I wouldn't have to worry about being seen in the windowless building.

I shone my light around. The space was narrow. The sides of the room were stacked full of something and covered with old, dark canvas tarps. I tried not to think of what could be under them. Skeletons of past retreat participants? A burble of nervous laughter rose in my throat.

In the center of the space was a small round table. Mismatched chairs, all of them old, skirted it. But it was what was in the center of the table that made me catch my breath.

I walked closer, shining the light beam directly toward the centerpiece. A silver tray, darkly tarnished, held six black taper candles. Around those were woven strands of silky ribbon and dead flowers. I shone the light beam closer and moved in for a better look. When I realized what I was looking at, I stepped back suddenly, nearly tripping over a chair. It scraped loudly over the floor.

It wasn't ribbon that was wound through the flowers but long lengths of hair. Human hair. Fingers trembling, I put out a hand toward it and then jerked it away. The thought of touching it—

I shivered, my stomach roiled. I swept the beam of light over the rest of the space. There was a strange-looking chair in the far corner. The back was high and ornate. Something enshrouded in plastic was perched in the middle of the seat.

I moved toward it, my sneakers unnaturally loud in the small space. Something scampered too close for comfort. I barely stopped myself from screaming as a field mouse ran over my foot. It dove into a hole in the floor on the other side of the room. Heart hammering in my chest, I swallowed hard.

Finally, I reached the chair. Under my fingers, the plastic was thick and heavy, like the kind that sturdy garbage bags are made from. I put my flashlight on the seat of the chair so I could open the plastic. It was pulled tightly around something square and hard. My hands shook slightly as I unwrapped a metal box. I let the plastic fall away and squatted, using the chair to balance the box while I opened its lid. Once it had contained "Auntie May's Delicious Country Cookies," but the label was faded and worn.

I pulled hard and the metal edges gave way. What could be inside? I pictured bones, spiders, or something equally horrifying. More human hair? Teeth? A skull? I shone the flashlight inside. My next breath came in a relieved whoosh.

Books.

A stack of three. I laughed weakly and reached for them. The first had a dark, tattered cover and read, *On the Mind and Metaphysics*. The second was, *Life as God,* and the third, *Her Holy Power.* I turned the last one over in my hands. Was it a novel? Something about the first female pope maybe? Or maybe not. The subtitle read: *On Capturing the Mind: Honoring the Goddess Within.*

Well, so what? So, the women wanted to learn more about becoming leaders or claiming their feminine power. My aunts had read and shared a handful of this type of book when I was growing up: women who howled at the moon and embraced their inner feminine power.

I opened the last book in the stack and started to read. The first three paragraphs droned on in hyperbolic language about the *feminine power* and *right thinking,* and *creating an environment of higher vibrations.* A little *woo-woo* but not alarming. I riffled through the pages looking for meatier topics. In the middle on page one-hundred ninety-seven, I found this:

And so, it is not that the One raises herself up over the others, but rather that the true leader is unveiled and so being, celebrated. Through following her example, others too, are manifesting their power and celebrating their roles in the utopian experience. If not for the One, who would lead? Denying her power is harmful, even destructive to the core of the community. This community—one built on trust, love, and yes, loyalty to the One—is foundational for real change.

Dedication, the ability to express commitment and pledge one's undying allegiance to a cause, a Being greater than oneself is a central idea behind finding true meaning. And how to best go about this? Through the devotion to and belief—

"What are you doing?"

I gasped and blinked, reorienting myself.

Ruby stood at the door, her hands on her hips, fingers digging into the flesh there. A pink windbreaker with a pattern that resembled a stained-glass window stood in sharp contrast to the fury mottling her face.

"I—"

"Guests aren't allowed here." She motioned to the books. "All of this is private property. Please leave. Immediately."

I swallowed, my cheeks hot with embarrassment, and put the book down, then crossed the room. I hesitated. What about what I'd seen earlier? I tried to form the question, but her gaze bore into me. I felt breathless and disoriented.

"I'm sorry, I—"

"Please leave," she repeated. Her voice was low and controlled but anger radiated toward me.

Fleeing the icehouse, I retraced my steps to the main building. My flashlight was gone, left behind. I stumbled back to the Retreat Center with my hands out in front of me.

As I walked up the steps and entered the house, my heart continued to flutter madly in my chest like a caged bird seeking release. I hurried to my room, mind whirling. One question ran through my mind like a record spinning endlessly: *What was going on?*

Chapter Twelve

There was a knock on the door. I groaned and rose from the rocking chair. My body was stiff and unhappy. I must have dozed after the adrenaline had burned off.

I hesitated my hand on the knob, then turned it.

"You're late." George handed me a napkin rolled into a ball. "Didn't you hear your wake-up call?"

I shook my head.

"I got you a muffin since they're cleaning up from breakfast."

I motioned him into the room, closing the door firmly. I felt a momentary pang of embarrassment. The room had a trail of muddy footprints—now dried to dust—and my still-damp clothes strewn across it. My hair stuck to the side of my face and my clothes were rumpled.

"What did you find?"

I shivered, thinking about the contents of the icehouse. "Some weird stuff."

George's eyebrows raised.

"There were books on feminine power—new age-y stuff— black candles and, oh, get this: human hair."

"What?" His voice cracked and he cleared his throat. "Are you serious?"

"As a death threat."

He rubbed a hand over his perfectly smooth jaw and studied the wall on the opposite side of the room.

"Before I went into banking, I took some religion classes. I thought I was meant to be a pastor." He grinned sheepishly, but then his face turned serious. "This is bad."

I stared at him.

"They could have been having a séance and you found the aftermath." He exhaled and shook his head. "Or black magic maybe? I want to see it. I'll walk over after we've been dismissed to write independently."

I shook my head.

"That's not a good idea. Ruby caught me last night. She wasn't happy that I was in there. They must lock it during the day—"

A knock sounded at the same time the door swung open.

"Good morning."

Randi stood in the doorway.

"Flora, Venetia asked me to remind you of your one-on-one session with her. And George, I had a question for you about the last piece you read. Could you spare a moment?" She inclined her head toward the hallway. George glanced at me and followed her.

"See you later," he called back.

Their footsteps squeaked down the stairs as I stuffed most of the muffin in my mouth. After using the cold water in the pitcher and the lavender soap to wash up, I quickly changed clothes. I brushed my hair and pulled it into a messy bun, then grabbed my notebook and pen. Coffee. I needed coffee in the worst way.

My hands trembled as I knocked on the door marked office that was tucked next to the kitchen. What I saw when Venetia opened it wasn't at all what I'd expected. Rather than the rustic, post, and beam style of the interior of the rest of the Center, this space was plain, minimalistic.

The room was a perfect small square. Besides an antique writing desk tucked under the eaves, there were potted plants and an open area that held two yoga mats. Light shone in the tall windows. Across from that wall was a small wood stove that pumped heat into the room. Near that was a small table holding a vintage rotary-style phone.

Venetia turned from watering still more plants that sat on a low shelf in front of the windows. She set down her metal watering can and nodded to me with a small smile. Her eyes assessed me, taking in my sweater and jeans, the messy bun. Irrationally, I wondered if she could see a successful writer inside a person just by looking at him or her.

"Glad you're here, Flora. Please, join me on the mats."

Venetia motioned to the open floor, and I followed her, settling myself cross-legged on the mat opposite her. It was a little close for comfort. I wanted to readjust my position so I wasn't so close but stayed where I was. Were we going to start our coaching session with yoga? I wished suddenly I knew how to do it. The only exercise I got consisted of walking my neighbor's dog when they were on vacation and trips to the mailbox.

"I find it easier to read someone's aura when we sit in a more relaxed posture like this. You don't mind, do you?"

Yes.

"No, this is fine."

"Good." Venetia brought her hands to my shoulders and hovered them there. "Go ahead and close your eyes, Flora. Try to relax."

I hesitated, then put my notebook and pen on the mat beside me and shut my eyes.

It was silent in the office for several uncomfortable minutes. Venetia breathed slowly, deeply. Outside the window, I heard a crow caw.

"Relax, Flora," Venetia said again, her voice soft. "Match your breathing to mine."

I did. Within a few minutes, my shoulders lowered from my ears. After that, I felt the tightness in my belly unfurl. I hadn't even realized I'd been clenching those muscles.

"Now, without opening your eyes, tell me what your deepest pain is."

"My—what?"

"I know it might feel strange to you. But we write from the place of our deepest pain. Sharing yours, giving it an audible voice can do incredible things for your writing practice."

"I'm sorry, I'm not really comfortable—"

"Flora."

I opened my eyes.

Venetia studied me, a benign smile on her face. "Do you have trust issues?"

"I'm sorry," I repeated. My voice was stiff now, like when a telemarketer called, and you'd been expecting your best friend. "I—"

"Never mind," Venetia waved her hands over my head as though wafting away smoke. She settled her hands onto my shoulders. Their warmth permeated my thin cotton sweater and the t-shirt I wore beneath. "Ruby said you were a bit," she paused. "Inhibited."

I wasn't sure whether to laugh or choke with indignation. Because I hadn't wanted to undress in front of a stranger like a prisoner with a guard?

"I thought we were going to discuss my writing trajectory. That you'd give me feedback on my work and—"

"Yes, yes," Venetia's fingers gripped my shoulders a little tighter. "But first, I need to get into the essence of you. Who makes up Flora Rossi?"

I shivered a little.

"Do you know that in all the years I was a bestseller, I never once felt happy? Never felt true peace. The media lies to us all. It promises that if we just have a little more money, a little more success, a little more fame, then we'll be content. But we never are.

"True happiness, true peace can only be found by doing interior work. It's not fun. Or easy. But it is necessary for our spirits. Writers especially need that interior peace. There is no other way to find the true meaning of life than to go deep within, to uncover the hidden parts of ourselves and plumb them."

I didn't know what to say to that. But sitting still in this spot with my eyes closed, I thought. without wanting to, of the night of the accident. My whole life had changed forever, irrevocably, in one thirty-second interval.

"Yes. Now you're feeling something," Venetia breathed. "I can feel your body working through it. Let it out, Flora. Let go of that pain you've been carrying for so long. It won't go further than this room. Release it and see how light and free you feel. Your writing will change—will strengthen—I promise you."

Something wet dripped down my cheeks. Tears, I realized. I hadn't cried after that night, not at Nonna's funeral, not through the reading of the will or the endless trips to bring old clothes and miscellaneous pots and pans and other detritus of life to donation centers.

"What happened," Venetia asked again.

I shook my head. Sobs bubbled up inside and my shoulders trembled.

"I can't—I don't want to talk about it," my voice was a hoarse, barely audible whisper.

"It's okay," Venetia's voice was soothing. "You don't have to tell me now. Just keep the images in your mind and listen to my voice. I'm going to walk you through a powerful exercise that will transform this traumatic experience into something more manageable. How does that sound?"

"Okay." My body felt so loose and tired that it was a chore to remain seated. Venetia's hands—were they holding me up now? I wanted to open my eyes and check but was too exhausted. What was happening to me?

"Lay back, Flora," Venetia's hands guided me into a supine position on the mat. She sat above my head, gently massaging my temples. The hard floor beneath it bit into my shoulder blades but I barely felt it. It was like I was floating. Someone else must be here on this mat, in this room. Someone other than me. The thought floated out of my head dreamily, almost as soon as it had appeared.

"Now, I'm going to release you from this painful memory, Flora. Believe me, I understand how much you're hurting. When I arrived here at Idyll Weiss for the first time, I was broken, threatening to come undone. It wasn't just being in the public eye, not just the critics of my books. My marriage was collapsing. My health had declined to the point that I never thought I'd feel good again. I was exhausted, wrung out."

Her warm hands stroked my forehead, once, twice, three

times. Then they settled over my eyes.

She began to rock a little, the motion, in turn, making my body follow. She hummed some tune I didn't recognize, then began to chant softly. I couldn't make out the words at first. When I did, I realized they weren't English. They were soothing though. My entire body sank into the mat beneath me, tension and pain seeping out into the hardwood floor holding me up. I wondered briefly what the words meant. Then why I cared. One word I did recognize: mother. Venetia would chant something, hum a few lines, then repeat "mother" once, twice, three times.

My body felt light and free. The near-constant ache in my head from tension was released. The sadness and grief that I wore like a blanket around my shoulders lifted. I didn't want to move. I never wanted this to end. A peaceful, white light enveloped me. I released a sigh unintentionally and Venetia hummed in response.

Minutes later—or had it been hours?—the motion slowed. Venetia stopped rocking. Eventually, she removed her hands from my eyes. I opened them. The room around me was too bright, the hard lines of the ceiling jarring. In my resting state, everything had been soft, warm, and comforting. Like being swaddled as a baby and resting in a parent's loving arms. Now I felt instantly cold. And alone.

"How was that?" Venetia smiled slightly.

"Wonderful," I responded. "Like getting a massage for your soul."

She threw her head back and laughed. "I like it. Maybe I'll include that on our next brochure."

Motioning for me to sit up, she placed a hand on my knee. We sat cross-legged now, across from each other. Our knees touched but now I felt no desire to move away.

"Flora, I hope you'll consider telling me about that pain in your past while you're here. This is a safe space. I wish I could convince you of the importance of getting that out into the open. Deep distress like that—can fuel our writing. But it can also ruin it, and rot away our creativity. Don't let that happen to you."

I forced a smile. It would feel good. To tell someone about it. I'd been working with Monica for what—six months?—and we still hadn't opened that box. My choice, not hers.

"I'll think about it."

Venetia smiled back and got to her feet. "I hope this has been helpful to you. And you know what? I would be willing to meet with you again before the retreat is over. To work through some of that with you. You just say the word."

"Thank you."

"Now, let's take a look at some of your work, shall we?"

Chapter Thirteen

The meeting room was icy cold when I walked in for the afternoon session. Imani rubbed her hands vigorously over her arms and scowled. Liam was pulling a sweater—a big, fisherman's one—over his flannel shirt. George grinned at me and motioned blowing on his hands as Randi shut the door.

As soon as I sat down, the door opened. I glanced up. Gwen hesitated in the doorway then walked to her seat without looking at anyone.

If a giraffe had walked through the door, I wouldn't have been more surprised.

"Gwen!" My voice was louder than I'd meant it to be. "You're here. You're *here*."

Imani looked at me strangely.

"It's just . . . I mean, is everything okay? With your family?"

Gwen gave a small smile. "False alarm. Everything is fine."

Randi clapped her hands together. "Sorry about the temperature." She rubbed her hands together briskly and made eye contact with each of us. "Flora, I'd told everyone earlier that a repairman was on the way. A pump broke on the solar system of our furnace so it's not circulating the heat the way it should."

Her gaze lingered on me. Did I imagine it or did her smile falter? Ruby must have told her she'd found me poking around in the icehouse. Randi turned toward the whiteboard that was set up behind her.

I doodled in my notebook, barely registering the lesson on how to overcome resistance to your writing practice. Instead, I spent most of the session thinking about the incredibly wonderful but strange experience in Venetia's office and sneaking glances at Gwen.

She seemed subdued but normal. Not frantic and terrified like she'd been yesterday. She answered questions posed to her and even smiled at a few of the comments people made. Still, something was off. It was like she was playing a role, pretending to be a version of her earlier self. Or was I imagining it?

Imani's words came to me: how we were creating drama that would be better captured in our writing. Is that what this was? Lots of writers struggled with mental health issues—depression, anxiety, and more. Many of us used our writing to explore these. Others of us rode the high we got from creating alternate worlds and realities, rode the power trip of having some semblance of control in lives that otherwise felt uncontrollable. Other writers found stories in the people and events around us as a way for our hungry brains to get their fix. Especially when the creative muse had fled. Is that what I was doing?

I tried to focus on what was being said about plot structure and detriments to our writing voice. Still, when Randi invited us to spread out around the house for the first activity, I immediately cornered Gwen in the dining room.

"Oh, hello," her voice was soft, her eyes didn't quite meet mine. "Sorry for the misunderstanding yesterday."

"Misunderstanding?" I hadn't meant for my voice to sound

so incredulous. I cleared my throat. "It was more than that. What's going on? I thought you said—"

"Just some miscommunication from home. We thought it was a family emergency, but it turned out not to be." She smoothed a hand over her dreadlocks. "Sorry to have worried everyone."

"So, everything's fine?"

She nodded.

"And you don't need a ride?"

"Ride?"

"A ride to town? Remember you—"

"Oh. No." Her voice was flat. "No, it was nothing. I was overreacting to some criticism over my work."

"Gwen," I put my fingertips on her forearm. "Are you sure you're okay?"

She smiled but it looked anemic. "Fine." She moved toward the door. "I forgot my pen in the meeting room. I think I'll just work there actually. See you later."

I stared after her, realizing seconds after she'd left that there had been a pen tucked into the wire spiral of her notebook.

Chapter Fourteen

"'Scuse me," a voice said behind me. I turned in the narrow hallway. A man in a stained canvas shirt with a logo on the breast pocket stood waiting to get by. He carried a bucket full of supplies that looked equally grimy.

"Sorry," I moved back slightly to allow him room to pass.

"I'm Blue." He had a thick French accent. He set down the bucket and stuck out a calloused hand. "Blue's Plumbing and Heating," he jerked his head toward the still-open front door where a banged-up blue van idled. He wore exceptionally thick glasses that made his eyes look googly. But his smile was friendly.

"I'm Flora. I'm here for the retreat." I shook his hand. "Nice to meet you."

Excitement fluttered in my chest. A local had just been dropped into my lap. If anyone knew about the Center and any strange things going on here, surely it would be someone from the area. But how could I fit that into polite conversation?

Screw it. I didn't have time for social niceties. This might be the only chance I had to talk to someone from the area.

"It's a beautiful place, isn't it?" I plunged on before he could answer. "Very unique. Although there have been some . . . well. Have you heard of anything," I lowered my voice. "You know, weird? About this property, I mean."

He puffed out his cheeks, looked down the hall both ways, then back at me.

"Weird." He scratched his neck just below the collar of his coveralls. "Well, girl, you know. People talk."

I nodded. "What do they say?"

"Just—"

"Mr. Blue," Ruby's voice sharply interrupted. "You remember your way to the basement, don't you?"

I took an involuntary step back from the plumber.

Blue nodded, that same big smile splitting his face. "*Oui.* Yes, madam. And it's just Blue." He moved off toward a door at the very end of the hallway.

"I hope you don't intend to leave your van idling the whole time you're here," Ruby called after him. "Mr. Blue? That van is spewing out toxic fumes into the environment. The state has a law against idling vehicles."

Blue called something back unintelligible, his feet thumping down the stairs. Ruby shook her head and mumbled something under her breath. She walked past me as though I wasn't there and out the front door. Climbing inside the van she turned it off, leaving Blue's keys on the front seat. As she moved off across the yard, calling to someone, I wondered what the plumber had been about to say.

I could follow him. See what he knew about Idyll Weiss.

Or maybe not. What you need to do is forget all of this. You realize this is just another form of procrastination, don't you?

Guilt spread across my midsection. I was wasting time, the precious days that were supposed to be carved out for writing my book. I thought this retreat was exactly what I needed. A chance to get away from all distractions and just write. Instead,

I'd spent most of it chasing shadows and avoiding the page.

Still, questions circled like hungry crows in my brain. What did Blue mean about the townspeople talking? And did it have anything to do with what I'd seen last night? The things I'd found in the icehouse?

Ignoring the little voice in my head haranguing me, I slipped down the basement staircase. The air was musty and smelled thickly of old earth. The steps were wooden and old, each one made from thick, uneven boards. I descended slowly, clutched the rough railing with my free hand, the other still wrapped tightly around my notebook.

"Blue?" I asked the empty space. Shadows danced and gyrated against the walls, and I could tell by the way it felt that the room was empty. I juggled my notebook and held out my cell phone, its little flashlight bright in the dark space. Three walls around me were stacked with sturdy-looking wooden shelves loaded with canned goods. Not tin-canned ones, but home-canned produce, neatly arranged in glass jars with dusty gold-rimmed lids. Barrels and metal tubs formed lines on a raised wooden platform beneath the shelves. The floor itself was made of packed dirt.

Bang! I jumped, my heart thundering in my chest. Ahead of me, a light flickered through another doorway. I walked that way, staying close to the fieldstone wall. When I got closer, I doused the light in my shirt. What if it wasn't Blue but one of the instructors? I didn't want to have to explain what I was doing down here.

A man's voice muttered, then a grunt and another bang— metal on metal. I poked my head into the space. Blue was bent over a shiny metal box halfway up the wall. He grumbled something under his breath in French. I'd learned enough in high school to get the gist.

"Blue?"

My voice was soft but he whirled around as though I'd yelled his name.

"Eh? Trying to give me a heart attack, girl?" He chuckled though. "Well, I need a good scare now and then; keeps me on my toes. You hold on one second . . ." He concentrated on whatever it was he was doing with the pipes in front of him. His tongue poked between his teeth and that, combined with the way his glasses made his eyes magnified behind the thick glasses nearly made me laugh.

"There." With his accent, it sounded like *dare*. He set down the tool in his hand, swiped a hand over his forehead, and wiped it on his dirty pants. "Just like I suspected. Needs a new thingamajig."

"Is that a professional diagnosis?"

He chuckled again. "Ayup."

"I was just wondering—"

"You was wondering what I meant 'bout what people in town say about this place."

I nodded. The wire binding of my notebook bit into my fingers.

He blew out a breath, his cheeks puffing out.

"You know, I shouldn't say nothing. It's money for me even if it ain't regular or—" He glanced from me to the box on the wall and back. "Convenient. But I don't much give two figs at my age. Nearing retirement—should have quit years ago, to tell de truth. But then Jamie moved back home and ran up some of our cards . . . well, girl." He surveyed me. "If I tell you you'll keep your lips zipped, eh?"

I nodded.

He lowered his voice and glanced around as though the instructors lurked in the shadowy corners.

"Remember, people say lots of stuff. Don't make it true. But dis place, it always been a little—how you say?" He paused, looking over my shoulder. "Ah. I dunno. But strange you know? Odd."

I nodded, encouraging him to go on.

"People own dis place before this group was—" he paused and made a whirling motion with his finger near his head. "My family, we moved here just thirty years ago—from Quebec." His shoulders straightened a little under his grease-stained shirt. "We keep ourselves to ourselves, eh?"

I nodded again.

"But there always been stories 'bout what goes on up here. Way I heard, few people gone missing over the years."

"From here—from the Retreat Center?"

Blue nodded. "Mmm."

"How many? When?"

He shrugged. "A few a long time ago. Last one about seven or eight years ago. Girl came to one of these meetings but never went back home. No one ever seen her again, far as I know."

"But there must have been an investigation?"

"Yup. But nothing ever found. They," he pointed up above us, indicating, I guessed, the retreat leaders. "Said she ain't never arrived. Her family hired some hotshot lawyer but he never found nothing."

"What was her name?"

"Eh? I dunno."

"Well, maybe she didn't. Ever get here."

"Maybe." Blue's bushy eyebrows pulled together. "And there

was others too. Maybe in the sixties, seventies, there were others," he repeated.

I shivered suddenly.

"Eh, it's just talk, you know. People, they like to gossip. My wife's one of 'em. And now, girl," Blue grinned. "I get back to my work. Otherwise, there won't be no bacon for Mrs. Blue to fry up in the pan. She's not going to be happy 'bout dat. You eat poutine?"

I shook my head slowly, wanting to ask him more about the woman who'd gone missing. But Blue had been distracted by the thought of the Quebecois dish—greasy fries smothered in gravy and dotted with cheese curds. He patted his robust belly.

"Poutine with crispy bacon, girl. You try dat," he smacked his lips. "You won't be sorry."

I forced a smile. "Okay. Well, thanks for the information."

"It's just talk. Long winters breed long tongues, that's what my *Memere* used to say. I ain't had no trouble with them myself." He took up another tool and moved back to the box. "It's a good thing, too, 'cause I need lots of dat bacon."

He tapped a tool to his hat's brim and nodded. I thanked him again and retraced my steps back toward the stairs. I moved slowly, careful not to trip.

But my mind whirled.

Chapter Fifteen

"There you are." The voice above my head was annoyed.

I glanced up from the window seat. I'd been sitting with my knees drawn up, staring out the window, notebook neglected beside me. Imani stood nearby, her lips pulled down.

"We're partners, remember? At the gong, we were supposed to find each other back in the meeting room and do the character role-play activity?"

Venetia had said something about this during the second-morning session, but it had been background noise as I puzzled over what Blue had told me.

"Right, sorry. I was lost in a daydream."

"Well, I hope it was about your character."

"Yeah. Of course." I forced a smile. What were we supposed to be doing? I stood up and gathered my notebook and pen. "Did you want to work inside or out?"

"In." Imani made a face at the nearby window. The wind blew and howled around the eaves of the house. The sound was a cross between a whistle and a moan. Tree branches crashed into each other, then leaped away as though they'd been burned. Dark clouds pressed down heavily and moved quickly across the expanse of sky. I wasn't sure how long I'd been staring out the window, but I hadn't seen any of this.

I followed Imani's straight back to a little nook in the corner of a small room near the dining area. It was dimly lit but cozy, a fire crackled cheerfully in the grate of the large, fieldstone fireplace.

"I'm surprised no one grabbed this spot." I settled into a Britton chair across from Imani.

"Oh, they tried. I told them it was taken."

I crossed my legs and then uncrossed them. I couldn't get my mind off Blue and what he'd told me. I considered asking Imani what she thought. I glanced at her and changed my mind. She looked at me with . . . what exactly? Disgust?

"Is something wrong?" I planted my feet on the floor and leaned toward her.

She shook her head, the edges of her bright scarf fluttered slightly.

"Let's just get started, okay?"

"I just wondered—"

"Yes?" Her voice was impatient, dark eyes boring into mine.

I cleared my throat. "Nothing."

"Good. So, tell me about the character you'll be playing." Imani folded her hands over her journal. "What is she or he like?"

I fumbled with my notebook, fingers flipping through blank page after blank page. I stared at them and frowned as though concentrating hard on the text there.

"You know what? I'm going to do this improv."

"Be my guest."

I paced for a few seconds, tried to remember what the heck this whole exercise was about but came up blank. I sat back down.

"Look, Imani. The truth is that I haven't had time to do a

character sketch. I was talking to . . . to someone and he told me some strange things about this place. He said—"

"No, uh-uh." Imani shook her head, her gold earrings twinkled in the firelight. "I'm not interested. I know you and that other guy—George?—have been messing around, playing Sherlock but I'm here to write. I don't understand you, people." She snorted softly.

"'You people'?"

"It's obvious this experience means nothing to you but it does to me. I take my writing seriously. I'm taking this *opportunity* seriously. But it's like this is all a game to you. Have you completed a single assignment since we've been here? I see you here and there and everywhere but never actually writing. Never working. This retreat—this is something I've dreamed of and worked for—for a long time. I've dreamed of writing books since I was a kid. And maybe opportunities like this come easily for you, but not for me. I have had to work hard for every single one I've been given. I'm not going to blow it like you. Just leave me out of all that."

"But I think—"

She held up a hand. "Not interested. Now, can you please be quiet long enough for me to share my writing?"

I sank back into the chair, deflated.

Imani rose and started to pace in front of the fire. She fingered through the pages of her notebook, then paused, looking suddenly to a spot behind my left shoulder.

"You!" Her voice was deadly calm and laced with anger. "You are the one."

A cold prickle ran down my back.

"You couldn't have me and wanted to make sure no one else would want me. You are the one who destroyed me."

Imani's eyes were narrow and filled with—what? Revulsion? Hatred? My hands clenched the arms of the chair so hard that I couldn't feel the difference between the silky material and my palms anymore.

"You ruined me," Imani's voice was husky, so low it didn't even sound female anymore. She put a hand to her throat and made a moaning sound. Then she staggered once, twice toward whomever she was looking at. I shot up out of the chair, expecting to see someone behind us waving a gun or brandishing a knife.

Imani gasped and collapsed, falling to the library's floor in a cloud of brightly colored fabric, and then lay still. I hurried to her side, shook her shoulder.

"Imani? Are you—"

"It's all because of you." Her voice was so quiet I had to bend close to hear it before it drifted away completely. Her eyes closed and she made a sound that was like a strangled moan.

"Imani?" I shook her harder and rolled her to her back. I was trembling as I put my fingers on her neck.

Her eyes popped open and she smiled at me, a catlike grin that made her eyes crinkle. It was the first time I'd seen a real smile since we'd been here. She sat up and I sat back on my heels and stared at her.

"What was that?" My voice was clipped. "You scared me."

She raised her hands over her head and stretched, letting out a long, satisfied sigh. "Well then, my job here is done."

I got to my feet, anger pinching my chest.

She stood too. "Character sketches, remember?" This was of my protagonist, Hany. She was a slave in Georgia, her life ruined by her traitorous fiancée, Benjamin, who impregnated her and—"

"I thought—you scared me," I repeated myself stupidly.

"You like that, don't you? Being scared."

"What's that supposed to mean?"

Imani crossed back to her seat and sat down, her back straight, her face smooth of all emotion.

"Isn't that why you're peeking around corners, making up stories about the people here? You love all that drama. Don't you?"

I was glad my arms were crossed so that I wouldn't smack her. "No." My voice was tight and small.

The fire popped. I glanced at it, away from Imani's penetrating gaze.

"Come on, Flora. Everyone's thinking it, but I'm the only one bold enough to say it. Maybe you shouldn't have come." She glanced from me to the fire and back again. "If you're just going to throw this gift back in their faces."

"Whose faces?"

"The retreat leaders; who else? They've given you—us—this incredible opportunity. And you're wasting it. Looking for ghosts and ghouls and skeletons in closets that aren't even there."

Imani stood, her silky clothes falling like a waterfall around her body. "Sorry, but I tell the truth where I see it."

I couldn't find a single word to say as she swept out of the room, leaving me behind with only the crackling fire and a hot, sick feeling in my stomach.

She was wrong.

I wasn't avoiding my writing work, there were just more pressing things at stake. *But what's happening here really?*

I'd met an odd young woman who could have mental health problems. I'd found a little building with some creepy items in it. So what? Maybe the retreat leaders liked dressing up and playing Halloween games or they had some sort of religious beliefs that were untraditional. That didn't make them evil. It didn't even make them suspicious. For that to be the case, there would have to have been a crime. An actual crime. Not some gossip that the locals made up.

I sank back into my chair. All my energy had leaked out. In its place my head started to pound, a central point between my eyes. I rubbed it.

This was it. My wake-up call. Maybe Imani hadn't delivered it kindly, but I'd gotten the message. Stop. Stop messing around. Quit trying to find mysteries that weren't there. A few weeks ago, I'd been over the moon excited about this opportunity. I'd never have imagined then that I'd be following a plumber around the building or sneaking out in the night to search the property of our hosts.

I straightened my shoulders, took a deep breath. This opportunity would only come around once and I needed to make progress on my book during this retreat. Shut out the distractions. Focus and, like Imani said, be grateful for the opportunity we had.

I stood and gathered my notebook. I'd go out to the sheltered front porch. The fresh air would help me tackle this writing assignment with a ferocity that left no room for anything but words.

I shrugged into my windbreaker and walked out onto the portico. The wooden sides of the porch kept out the rain but still allowed a great view of the storm in full swing. I'd just closed the door behind me when I heard what sounded like a scream.

My head jerked up and I looked around me.

Nothing.

Maybe it had just been the wind. Bare branches overhead click-clacked together like someone drumming long finger-nails on a smooth surface.

I sat down on one of the plain wooden chairs and took out my pen.

Seconds later, the front door banged open. I jumped, turning so fast that the chair nearly tipped over. Ruby, flushed and upset-looking, ran out the door. She wasn't wearing a jacket and her t-shirt was instantly soaked as she ran down the steps and across the yard.

"Ruby? What's the matter?" I called after her. "Ruby?"

She ignored me or didn't hear me and disappeared around the side of the barn. *This doesn't concern you. Ruby's a big girl, she can take care of herself.*

I stared at the sheets of rain and thought of my editor, Jane, and her displeasure the last time we'd talked. Of her veiled threat that if I didn't have something—and something good— produced by the end of this grace period another author could easily fit into my spot in the production lineup.

But knowing something in your head and your heart are two very different things.

I ran after Ruby.

Chapter Sixteen

Ruby was outside the barn, leaning up against the rail fence, gasping. Her cheeks which had been flushed moments before were china-plate white. Her eyes, dazed-looking, stared past my shoulder out into the gardens.

"Ruby?" I shouted above the wind. "Are you okay?"

She didn't acknowledge me.

"Ruby?" I touched her arm. She jerked back as though I'd burned her. She looked at me then, worked her mouth up and down. I thought of Old Marley's ghost in *The Christmas Carol*, trying to get his jaws to work.

"Don't let—" The wind snatched her words which had been little more than a croak. She collapsed, crumpling into the mud like a doll in slow motion.

"Ruby." I bent down, grabbed her shoulders. "Help! Someone, please help. Call nine one one."

My brain felt as though someone had stuck a whisk in my skull and started scrambling. What do you do in emergencies like this? I'd never taken CPR. *Think. think.* Choking people were put on their sides, weren't they? I turned Ruby onto her side. A tiny dribble of blood ran down the side of her neck. Above the red trickle was a tiny blur of yellow. I put my finger there. What was that? Something fluffy and soft on top of her skin. But underneath it, something hard protruded. Rain streamed down my face, blinding me.

I swiped at my eyes, trying to see more clearly. Ruby's loose hair was plastered around her face and neck. I pushed it away, trying to get a better look.

A hand grabbed my arm hard. "What happened?" Randi yelled.

"I don't know."

She pushed me aside with her slim frame, blocking my view as she bent over Ruby. I wrapped my arms around my waist, shivering.

"Come on, Ruby. Come on." Randi slapped her face gently, then more forcefully. She put a finger alongside her neck, checking for a pulse. She waited a few seconds, then moved it a little to the left and then to the right.

Randi looked up. "Go and get Venetia."

"Is she—" I nodded toward Ruby. "Is—"

"Hurry." Rain ran down Randi's face in streams.

I stumbled away from them backward a few steps, before turning and running as fast as I could. I should have asked her about the thing in Ruby's neck. What had it been? Maybe fuzz from her clothes, or a piece of string that had stuck there. But then the hard thing under my fingertips—

Abruptly. I stopped. Mud oozed into my shoes and rain pelted my head and face. I remembered a nature show about primitive hunting practices that were still used in many parts of the world. Blowguns fashioned from wood shot out tiny but deadly poisoned darts. But that didn't make any sense. Not here. My stomach twisted and I started running again. Ruby needed an ambulance.

My feet pounded up the front steps like explosions. I banged through the door, eying the interior wildly.

"Venetia?" My voice echoed in the narrow wooden hallway. "Venetia?" I tripped over an overturned rainboot and ran toward the meeting room. Bursting through the door, my breath came in ragged gasps. Five sets of eyes turned toward me.

"Venetia, hurry. Ruby—she's . . . she needs help. Call for an ambulance." My voice wobbled then broke.

Voices gasped and the faces around the table wore various expressions of shock and surprise. Except one. Gwen's face was as still and impassive as it had been the last time that I'd seen her.

Venetia shot out of her seat and ran to me. She gripped my arms, fingers biting into the flesh. "Where?"

I motioned toward the open door. "By the barn. Randi is with her. You need to call—"

But she was already gone. I stared at the open door.

"Someone needs to call an ambulance," I addressed the blank faces. "We should . . ."

The edges of my vision formed a tunnel. Grayness pressed in. Someone's voice from far away asked if I was all right.

And then everything went black.

Chapter Seventeen

I had strange, scattered dreams that left me hot and thirsty. When I opened my eyes again, I was lying in my room, on top of the white coverlet. My head throbbed and my tongue felt soldered to the roof of my mouth. I tried several times without success to speak.

". . . water?" I finally croaked out.

The fabric near the head of my bed whispered together. I tried to turn my head that way but the pain in my head intensified, radiating into my neck.

"Here. I'll lift your head and then you can sip this," Imani's face came into focus, and she looked me over, her brow creased with worried wrinkles. "You scared us."

"I . . ." *Ruby.* Was she dead? What had happened? How long had I been unconscious? I glanced toward the window but the curtains were closed.

"It's just past three." Imani lifted my head and pressed smooth glass to my lips. I sucked at it greedily before the water hit my tongue. I drank deeply, then she lowered my head gently back onto the pillow.

"Is Ruby okay?"

Imani avoided my eyes.

"Imani?"

"She didn't make it."

"The ambulance?"

"The phone is out. Venetia thinks that a tree took the lines down."

I stared at the ceiling. My brain felt coated with molasses, sticky and slow.

"What . . . happened to me?"

"You fainted. Don't you remember anything?"

I tried shaking my head but quickly realized that wasn't possible.

"You hit your head on the table on the way down."

She lifted my eyelids gently one by one and shone a light into each eye, making them instantly water uncontrollably. "I don't think you have a concussion. But I bet you have a massive headache."

I smiled faintly.

"Try not to move too much."

"How do you know I don't have a concussion?" My voice was a little louder but still froggy-sounding.

"I'm a school nurse." She smiled at me and it transformed her face.

"Randi gave you an herbal tincture. It's supposed to help with any internal swelling. It smelled like death and didn't look much better. I guess it's a blessing you were out cold when she administered it."

"Randi?" My head started to clear slightly. An image of Randi bending over Ruby's prone body formed. The room started to tip again, but I forced myself to breathe slowly. I'd never passed out before. I'd rather not repeat the process anytime soon.

"You need to rest. There's nothing to do now anyway but

wait. Someone made tea. I could get you some. Or are you hungry?"

"No, thanks."

"If you change your mind, there are leftovers from breakfast. People are just mindlessly eating, probably to get their minds off the—" she stood abruptly and smoothed down the silky fabric of her tunic.

The what? I almost asked and then realized what she'd been about to say. To get their minds off the dead body in the house. Where had they put Ruby? I shivered, the quilt around me not thick enough.

"Can I get you anything else?"

"More water, please."

She patiently repeated the process from earlier. Where had this new Imani come from? I could see how good she must be with her students.

"I'll refill the pitcher and leave it by your bed."

"Thank you."

She returned several minutes later with a freshly topped-off glass and a small, brown pitcher. She put both on the table and retreated.

"Try to get some more rest. You'll feel better when you wake up."

I said I would but didn't plan to stay in bed. I'd wait until she'd left then get up and find out what was going on.

Except whatever Randi had given me made my body feel like lead and my brain like mush. Getting out of bed seemed laughable.

Soon, I was pulled back into darkness.

Chapter Eighteen

When I woke up next, the room was very dark. Earlier, the storm had been loud. Now, the wind sounded frantic. It tore at the siding and yanked on the eaves. The wood creaked and groaned. Thunder grumbled and rain slashed at the window. Occasionally but too often for comfort, there was a distinct cracking sound of branches falling. I imagined a giant one falling onto the house, crushing me in my bed.

The thought motivated me to push myself up. I went slow. My head felt better, more of a dull drumbeat now than a pounding hammer. I stumbled against the nightstand but couldn't find a candle or my phone. Someone—Imani?—had taken off my wet clothes. It was hung to dry on the back of the chair. I wore a nightgown, thick socks, and my underthings.

Fumbling with the dresser drawers, I located fresh jeans and a hoodie. I'd just bent over to retrieve a pair of socks that had fallen from my fingers when I found my cellphone, partially hidden under the bureau. I quickly flicked on the light and made my way to the door. The porcelain knob was icy under my hand.

The door swung inward quickly, nearly hitting me in the head. I gasped. A blinding light seared my eyes.

"Sorry." A man's voice. The light faded.

I blinked a few times, seeing blue squiggles in the now-dim light.

"Are you all right?" It was George.

"I guess so. I've felt better but at least I'm not . . ." I cleared my throat, the unspoken word hanging in the air between us. I turned off the light on my phone. It didn't have much battery left and I wanted to save it.

"We've been worried." He lifted the lantern back up to chest level. The yellow light dripped and puddled onto the floor, casting strange jumping shadows on our faces.

"We're all downstairs and have been taking turns checking on you every thirty minutes. We probably should have just set you up on the couch down there, but Venetia thought you'd be more comfortable in your room."

I nodded slowly.

"Do you want to come down?"

"Yes." The thought of other people, light, and warmth was overwhelmingly appealing suddenly.

"Can you make it down the stairs? I can help."

I said I could, and he took my arm like I was his grandmother, leading me slowly down the hallway and then the squeaky stairs.

"The phone is out but the storm can't last much longer." His voice had a forced cheerfulness to it.

"Really?"

The wind outside sounded worse as we descended, like a wild thing trying to get in.

"It's been raging like this for a long time. Almost feels like the tail end of a hurricane but it's too late in the year for that. Anyway, I haven't heard of any passing through the States or the Caribbean. Have you? Sorry," he paused, and I bumped into him. "I talk too much when I'm nervous."

"Along with eating chocolate?"

George laughed but then sighed loudly. "I'm nearly out."

"Is everyone else okay?"

I saw George nod out of the corner of my eye. He waited for me to start moving again before he spoke.

"As okay as they can be. The instructors are all upset—we all are—but no one else was hurt or anything. So, at least there's that."

"How long do you think before the phone is working again?"

George shook his head, the light from the lantern making his face ghoulish.

"I'm not sure. They think maybe a tree went down somewhere between here and the road. Probably a lot of somewheres actually, so it could be a while. But it's fine. Venetia assured us that we won't run out of food or water or anything."

Ruby's face, as white as cotton, played in my mind. I suddenly wanted to tell George what I'd seen. But was it really a dart? A shudder ran through my body. But if it was and we were all trapped here, in the middle of nowhere with a killer, shouldn't I tell the rest of them?

"George," I squeezed his arm. "I'm not sure that Ruby's death was an accident."

"What?"

His voice was too loud in the quiet space and I shushed him.

"What do you mean?"

"I saw her before . . . when she collapsed. She ran out of the house like she was on fire. And when she fell by the barn, there was blood—"

"There's the patient." A loud voice interrupted.

Venetia's concerned face looked up at us from the bottom of

the staircase. "No worse for the wear, I hope?"

I forced a small smile. "I'm fine, thanks."

"That's what we like to hear. I'll get you both some tea."

George shot me a look as we followed Venetia into the dining room, his arm still under mine.

"It seems we always end up here, surrounded by food," Randi was saying as we entered the room. "Whenever there's a celebration or a tragedy, food is the answer."

"Not the answer." Venetia filled two mugs with streams of steaming tea. "Just a distraction."

Randi nodded but her face looked closed off. She pushed away that plate containing a muffin that Venetia had placed beside her on the table. Everyone else was there, too: Liam, looking somber and even more handsome in the flattering candlelight, glanced up and smiled slightly when we entered.

Imani sat next to Gwen at a small table in the more shadowed part of the room. I searched Gwen's face, but she looked the same. Pale but calm. She glanced down at her plate, methodically picking up crumbs of something and depositing them onto another area of the plate.

George pulled a chair out for me near Liam then settled at a seat near Randi. Venetia handed him one of the mugs of tea. The other, she deposited in front of me. The steam bathed my face and the scent—bitter and earthy—was strangely reassuring. I smiled my thanks, but she'd already turned away.

"Feeling okay?" Liam's dark eyes studied me thoughtfully.

I nodded and stirred honey into the tea. A cloud of steam erupted from the mug. "Much better, thanks."

"What can I get you to eat?" Venetia asked from her spot by the makeshift buffet.

"I'm all right."

Imani and Randi talked quietly over Gwen's head and Venetia added something to her plate while answering a question George had asked her about her books.

"Crazy situation, isn't it?" Liam asked me after a few seconds.

I glanced at him again. His head was bent toward his plate, spooning something—bread pudding maybe?—into his mouth. He chewed and leaned back, his eyes studying me.

"Ruby?" I asked, the name sticking slightly on my tongue.

He nodded. "And this storm. Us being trapped here."

I nodded and sipped the tea. It scalded my lips. We were silent for a few long minutes, while conversation in a murmured hush flowed in the room. Paula joined us, settling her tall body heavily into a chair near Randi but not looking at her. She ignored everyone, staring directly across the room at the far wall.

Venetia seemed the most unaffected of all the instructors. She chuckled wryly at something George said, then nodded toward Randi with a smile. Randi didn't notice. She looked into her mug of tea as though searching for answers.

Imani asked Gwen something and she answered. I was too far away to hear what they were saying.

". . . body out of here."

"What's that?" I turned back to Liam, who rubbed a big cloth napkin over his mouth and leaned forward in his chair.

"I said I'll be glad when they get the body out of here."

"Me too. Where . . ."

Liam inclined his head toward the hallway. I did a quick mental map of the Retreat Center.

"The meeting room?"

He nodded. "Paula and Ruby shared a room. All the other rooms are full, so they put her in there. Randi said it was fitting.

But it is a little unnerving."

I tried to keep my expression neutral but a trickle of icy discomfort crept along my back. A dead person in the next room would unnerve a lot of people. Despite the discomfort, a question niggled. Could I somehow get in there, alone, to look at Ruby's neck?

Suddenly, inexplicably, my eyes filled with tears. I looked down at my hands, embarrassed, but Liam had already seen.

"Hey, are you sure you're all right?" He waited for a beat, then continued. "It must have been hard for you, finding her body."

"I didn't," I blinked hard twice. "I mean, she wasn't dead yet. When I found her . . . she was trying . . . trying to tell me something. But I couldn't understand her. And then—"

"More tea?" Venetia appeared by my arm, startling me.

"No, thank you," I instinctively put my palm over the mug and looked up at her. Closer up, I saw lines of strain around her eyes. Her lips, though, turned up in a small smile, seemed thin and pinched.

"Venetia, I'm sorry about Ruby. I'm sure it must be a shock."

"Sad but not a shock." She must have noticed my startled expression. "Ruby had a heart condition," she said softly. "And she didn't take care of herself the way she should have. So, it wasn't a surprise, per se. But it leaves a hole, doesn't it? You're never really prepared to lose someone." Her voice cracked and she blinked twice, hard.

"No, of course not. I'm sorry for your loss." The words sounded hollow and contrived in my ears.

"Thank you," Venetia cleared her throat and smiled a brittle-looking smile. "Did I already ask you if you wanted something to eat?"

"I'm fine, thank you."

"Maybe later. We'll leave the food out until everyone is ready to turn in," she said in a louder voice to everyone in the room. How long was everyone going to sit here? In daylight, it would be harder to get into the meeting room unobserved.

A gust of wind rattled the window panes, I jumped and so did Randi. The lantern light flickered. Bare branch tips *click-click-clicked* against the windows.

"Quite a storm," Liam said.

I nodded distractedly and sipped my tea. Was I going to sit here and discuss the weather, while Ruby's dead body lay just yards away? An image dropped into place in my mind—a streaky trickle of blood from her neck turning pink in the rain.

Suddenly there was a hot, uncomfortable band of pressure in my chest like I was trying to hold in a violent cough.

"Are you—" Liam started, but stopped when I drew my face inches from his.

"Don't ask me again if I'm okay. I'm not."

He raised his eyebrows and frowned.

"I need to see her," I whispered but it still sounded too loud in my ears.

"See her?"

"Ruby. I need . . . I need closure."

He didn't say anything, just sat and stared at me as though I'd morphed into something else. A toad maybe. Or a unicorn.

Hot frustration rose in my chest and climbed up my throat.

"Never mind." I stood and pushed my chair in. It hit the table and a little tea sloshed up over the side of the mug. A little wave of dizziness washed over me.

"Do you want me to go with you?" Liam whispered, standing close to me. His aftershave was woodsy.

Did I? I didn't like the idea of going into that room alone. But I didn't want Liam to know why I was really going. Maybe there was someone outside—a stranger who'd killed Ruby. But any one of us could have done it. While I couldn't picture quiet, well-spoken Liam as a murderer, it didn't mean he wasn't. The thought of entering the cold, dark room on my own made goosebumps run up and down my arms though.

I nodded to Liam. He quietly pushed his chair in, leaving his plate and mug neatly stacked. He took the candle in the old-fashioned holder from the table. He was so tall he had to duck to miss the lower candles on the ugly wooden chandelier overhead.

"I'm going to help Flora back to her room," Liam said.

"Yes, get some rest," Venetia's eyes followed us.

A single candle burned in a wall sconce in the dark hallway. I followed Liam, the weak candlelight barely illuminating the space. We paused outside the meeting room. The knob was icy under my palm. I hesitated.

"Is it locked?" Liam asked.

I shook my head. Twisting the doorknob, I took a breath as the door swung silently open.

Chapter Nineteen

Liam grabbed the door before it banged into the wall and closed it softly behind us. Dread trailed its long fingertips up my spine. The old phrase, *cold as a crypt,* was apt. The room was icy, silent, and dark.

"Do you have a flashlight?" Liam asked. "My phone died yesterday."

I pulled mine out of my sweater pocket, fumbling with the screen. I finally hit the flashlight button. A small stream of bright-white light made everything monochromatic like we'd just stepped into a black-and-white movie from the forties.

The large table, the chairs, and the small podium—everything had been pushed to the right side of the room. On the left was a cot. A body lay on it covered in a flowered sheet. I swallowed. *Hurry up! Get this over with.* My feet didn't respond though.

Finally, I took a deep breath and walked toward it. Liam's feet whispered on the floorboards behind me.

Standing in front of the lumpy shape, my heartbeat hammered in my ears. *Go back, go back, go back.* But it was too late now. I grasped the corner of the sheet and pulled it back. Ruby looked as though she'd been bleached by the sun, left too long exposed to its rays. Her hands were folded across her chest, like the other dead people I'd seen at wakes over the years. She looked a bit deflated but otherwise, as though she might open her eyes, sit up and ask us what had happened.

Liam cleared his throat. "Would you like a moment alone?"

"Yes. But please, don't leave."

"I'll wait by the door."

I nodded, my eyes already searching Ruby's pale neck. The lines and creases looked deeper in the anemic light. I closed my eyes for a second, thinking of how she'd been slumped and where I'd been standing. The spot was on her right side, maybe a couple of inches under her ear. I ran a fingertip lightly over the area. Her skin was icy and hard and I jerked back involuntarily. Then I braced myself and traced the area again. Disappointment bubbled in my chest. There was nothing. Except . . .

There.

A bump. Small and hard, just below the surface of the skin. I could pinch it, see if it moved with the skin. My hand shook. I tried to shift Ruby's head a little toward the wall, but rigor mortis had already set in.

The door opened with a creak. I twisted awkwardly from my crouched position and nearly fell over. Venetia stood in the doorway, her mouth a flat, angry line.

"What are you doing in here?"

I got to my feet and faced her.

"We were just saying our goodbyes." Liam stepped toward Venetia, partially blocking me from her razor-sharp gaze. "When Flora found Ruby she didn't have a chance to have any closure. We didn't mean to intrude, but you can imagine how hard this must be for Flora."

Venetia's face cleared and her voice softened.

"I know. It was very sudden. And then with you injuring yourself." She nodded toward me. "I find it hard to believe too. That she's really gone." Venetia looked at Ruby, but her face didn't crumple with tears or change really in any way. Instead, her stare was impassive, as though she was looking at one of the chickens in the yard or listening to one of our readings.

I opened my mouth but then closed it again. Until I knew for sure what had happened to Ruby, everyone was a suspect. It couldn't have been Venetia though—she was leading the class. I kept my suspicions to myself. Again, I considered whether there could be someone else on the property. Maybe someone the instructors didn't know about. Images of a man looking suspiciously like Ted Kaczynski appeared in my mind. Maybe it had been an accident. Someone was hunting using the old-school method and—

Stupid. No one would be hunting in a storm like that.

Venetia was looking at me strangely. I realized I'd been staring as my mind scrambled to make sense of the situation.

"I wish I'd gotten to her sooner," I said, filling in the gap. It was true. If I'd just found her a few minutes earlier, maybe she'd still be alive.

Venetia stepped closer. I thought she was about to hug me, but instead, she brushed past me to lean on the edge of Ruby's cot.

"Dear friend," she said quietly and pulled the flowered sheet up and over the still form. She sighed loudly. "Everyone is heading upstairs to bed. You two should as well."

Liam nodded. I felt strangely irritated. How could any of us possibly sleep?

"The storm will likely blow over before morning." Venetia turned to us. "And then everything will be back to normal.

Well . . ." She glanced apologetically toward the form on the cot. "As normal as it can be. I'll call the ambulance and police as soon as the line is fixed. I assume they'll send the coroner." She looked at something across the room.

I followed her gaze. A shadow moved past the door in the hallway.

"You should both get some rest."

"Venetia." I put my hand on her arm as she passed. "Is there anyone else here? At the Retreat Center, I mean. Like maintenance workers or housekeepers or anything?"

Venetia looked perplexed, the faint light from the hallway bouncing over the planes of her face. "No, not regularly. We do lease some of the property to small farmers—they sell specialty foods at a farmers' market—but they wouldn't be here in a storm."

"Oh."

"Why?" Did I just imagine that her voice sounded wary, guarded?

My throat suddenly felt dry.

"I just wondered. I . . . I thought I heard one of the other instructors mention that someone was coming. But they were probably talking about the phone techs or something, getting them out here tomorrow. Like you said."

She smiled but it didn't reach her eyes. "I'll see you in the morning."

Liam and I said goodnight to her and walked back toward our rooms. The stairs creaked under someone else's weight further ahead of us.

"What's really going on?" Liam's mouth was so close to my ear that his breath moved the hair there. "Why were you prodding Ruby's neck?"

I could lie. Tell him I hadn't been, that there had been an ant and I'd brushed it away. But the need to tell someone else what was going on was overwhelmingly strong.

"I think she was killed." My voice was a whisper but still felt conspicuously loud.

Silence.

I glanced at Liam. He'd stopped by the stairs, his dark eyes on mine when I turned to him.

"What?"

I told him what I'd seen out in the rain. What I'd been looking for on Ruby's neck.

He was quiet while I whispered all of this to him. Then he rubbed a hand over the stubble on his cheek and chin. His fingers were long and nicely shaped. I wondered absently if he played the piano.

"We should stick together." His voice was soft. "Does anyone else know?"

Creaks from the stairs above us were so loud they nearly drowned out his last words.

George knew about the icehouse. I summarized it for Liam. About the weird things I'd found there and the people we'd seen walking in the woods.

His eyes widened. "Whoever did this—you know it must be one of us."

A shiver skittered along the back of my neck like a spider.

"It could have been one of the farmers they lease land to," I said, liking that idea much better. I didn't mention my wild man theory though. It was too embarrassing to say out loud though I couldn't get the image of a figure dressed in animal skins out of my mind.

"Doubtful." Liam had reached the top of the stairs and turned in the direction opposite my room.

"Maybe we should go back to where Ruby . . . fell. See if we can find anything else." I wanted to snatch the words back and stuff them where they'd come from.

Liam nodded. My heart sank.

"When?"

"After everyone is asleep, I guess. And we should use the back door. Someone—Randi or Venetia—might be sitting up with the body all night like an old-fashioned wake." I held back a shudder.

Liam nodded.

"Which room are you in?"

He pointed to the last one on the left. A small window sat at the end of the hallway and through it, I could make out the ghostly shapes of trees swaying. An occasional sliver of moon appeared and disappeared as black clouds scurried across it. The storm must be breaking.

"I'll knock in about an hour," I whispered. "Everyone should be asleep by then."

He nodded and yawned.

I lifted my eyebrows.

His yawn turned into a chuckle. "I won't fall asleep."

Chapter Twenty

My room was cold and smelled faintly of lavender, dust, and the outdoors. I walked to the window. A thin band of frigid air poured in at the bottom casing. I shivered and rubbed my hands over my arms. Wrapping myself in a spare quilt, I sat in the upright chair and tried to focus my thoughts on something other than Ruby and poisoned darts, and a murderer in the house.

I failed miserably.

Waiting exactly an hour, I used my watch's stopwatch function to count down the last few seconds. I'd found a flashlight in the bureau, rolled to the back of the drawer. I tucked it into my jacket's pocket.

The idea of getting into my car and driving off bounced around in my mind as I tiptoed toward Liam's door. I pushed it away. Even if I could get back down the driveway—which was doubtful if trees had come down—what then? I still hadn't found my keys but prayed they were in the car. Even if they were though, would my car make it down the desolate dirt road in this storm? Being stranded here was scary. But being stranded out in the middle of nowhere in a car that was stuck was even worse.

Besides, if I left, how would I ever find out what happened

to Ruby?

I gave two light taps on Liam's door. Seconds later he emerged, rubbing his eyes.

"I lied," he said.

I smiled and he took the lead, maneuvering the normally creaking stairs with the grace of a cat. I followed his foot placement exactly and was surprised that we didn't make a sound.

He grinned over his shoulder at me when we reached the back door. "Years of practice at home," he whispered. "Made me a genius at memorizing the squeaky parts of staircases."

He eased open the door. The wind sucked at our clothes and hair, pulling, and snatching with cold fingers. I wrapped my jacket more tightly around myself. The flashlight was reassuring in my pocket.

I looked side to side but saw nothing other than violently bucking trees and eddies of leaves blowing everywhere. The rain had stopped at least, though droplets from branches overhead still sprayed down on our heads unexpectedly. Liam moved to flick on his flashlight, but I put my hand over it.

"Wait until we're a little further from the building."

He nodded.

A single puddle of warm light came from the meeting room when I glanced over my shoulder at the house. There was a wake then, taking place tonight. As chilly as it was outdoors, I was grateful to be here and not in the meeting room. I followed Liam to the main path and we both flicked on our lights.

"It was there." I pointed toward the barn where Ruby had fallen. "She ran out the front door and straight over there."

Liam blocked his face from the wind with his big hand and followed me. When we got to the spot, I shone the flashlight around the ground, on the posts of the fence that Ruby had clung to. I didn't know what we were looking for, maybe a rogue dart, a note she'd dropped, something to tell us what had happened.

But there was nothing. Any evidence would have been carried away by the wind or ruined by the rain hours ago or trampled in the mud under our feet. There were the faintest of boot tracks in the wet earth, but the earlier rain had mostly washed these away. I bent and inspected them anyway.

"See anything?" Liam's voice was quiet near my shoulder.

I shook my head. It hadn't been likely we'd find something. But I'd wanted so much to—

The beam of the flashlight snagged a bit of yellow poking out of the mud. Moving the light closer, I saw a tiny pinprick of yellow fluff. It was half wedged into one of the boot prints nearest the fence.

"Look!" My fingers reached toward it.

"Wait!" Liam handed me a plastic sandwich bag. "I used this for my razor. Brought it out just in case."

The wind tried to snatch it as he handed it to me. I put the baggie over my hand and picked up the bit of fluff. My hand froze when I tugged on it. A small, silver-pointed tip slipped out of the muddy footprint. I grasped it carefully and folded the bag backward over it. Then I stuck the whole thing into my pocket.

"Do you know what this means?" Liam's voice sounded excited.

I glanced at him.

He stared at my pocket. "She was murdered."

The word hung in the air between us.

A mixture of relief and a renewed sense of fear tangled in

my chest. Relief because I'd been right. And fear for the same reason.

"We should go." The wind whipped my words away.

We followed the fence back toward the house. We were nearly at the edge of it when a crack split the air. *Lightning.* But the storm was over. Where—

"Look out!" Liam grabbed my arm, jerking me to the right. A series of bangs and cracks sounded, like a packet of firecrackers going off. A huge limb from a nearby tree crashed to the ground where I'd stood seconds ago. The branch was almost as big around as my thigh. Bark shattered on impact, scattering debris over the ground, and crushing the corner of the fence.

I tried swallowing but my mouth was too pasty.

"Are you all right?" Without waiting for a reply, Liam propelled me into the barn.

The rain started again. It sounded like fingernails drumming on the tin roof. Inside, the barn smelled of old hay and the leftover fumes of oil or gasoline filled the space. I breathed deeply, shakily, and put a hand to my head, which pounded once again.

"Thank you." My voice shook. "I—"

"It's okay," Liam slid his hands over my arms. They were warm and strong and felt good there. Solid.

"I'm just glad I saw it in time."

I moved closer to him, drawing in his warmth like water after hours on the hot sand. He smelled piney and faintly— oddly—like the strange tea we'd been served since arriving here. He hesitated and then drew me closer.

I'm not sure what happened next—who moved where or when—but our faces were suddenly close, his breath warm on my cheek. I turned my face, or he turned his and our lips met.

The kiss was warm and soft, gentle. Even his lips were warm like the rest of him. It felt good, comforting, and safe.

Finally, we broke away from each other, the sound of our breathing muted in the big, empty space. The wind continued to howl and beat itself against everything outside the door. It was like an angry child having a tantrum—screaming and thrashing and being generally hysterical.

For some reason that image made me laugh. It bubbled up into a single, hiccupping gasp and then another and another until I was doubled over, my hands clamped over my mouth, tears streaming from my eyes.

Liam looked at me uncertainly, his eyebrows raised.

"I didn't think I was that out of practice."

That made me laugh even harder. I couldn't stop, couldn't breathe. I was horrified at myself. At best, he thought I was a lunatic. At worst, insulting his romantic gesture. But the harder I tried to stop the more the choking laughter and tears came.

Until, finally, it ended as suddenly as it had started.

Wiping my eyes on the edge of my t-shirt I glanced at Liam. He was looking at me as though I was crazy, which was exactly how I felt.

"I'm sorry." I cleared my throat and shoved the rest of the hysteria down. "That had nothing to do with you. It's just nerves. The stress of everything." I waved my hands through the air ineffectually.

Liam nodded but still looked confused. Who could blame him? It was probably the first time a woman had broken out in hysterics after he'd kissed her. The thought made more laughter bubble up, but I cleared my throat and looked away.

"Really, I am sorry. It's just—"

"It's all right." He gave a half smile. "It's been a long day and you've been through a lot. But we should get back." He nodded toward the house. "Before someone sees us."

I looked toward the Retreat Center. Its shape reminded me of an animal, crouched in the shadows waiting to pounce. I shook the thought away and nodded.

Together we ran, unsuccessfully avoiding puddles, not stopping until we came to the back door. I went in first and eased it open as noiselessly as I could. But as I turned to hold it for Liam, I saw something out of the corner of my eye out in the treeline. A flash of white.

A person in a white robe. I pointed soundlessly and Liam turned, saw the figure, and frowned. He started to go back the way we'd come, sticking close to the edge of the woods. I followed. My breath was jerky, my throat dry.

Who was it? And where—

I stopped, grabbing at Liam's jacket, which was slick with rain. He turned, a questioning look on his face.

I pointed silently and he followed my finger. The white robe had been joined by others shrouded in black. They walked in a single-file line, slowly, as though it were a perfectly beautiful evening and not the middle of a storm.

I jabbed my finger from the group to us and back again, hoping Liam would understand. He must have because he nodded and continued walking in the same direction but in a low crouch. I followed. We needed answers.

But after this, I was getting out of here, storm or not. I'd take my chances on the road. A cold raindrop plopped on the back of my neck and slid icily down my spine.

Goosebumps ran up my arms as I followed Liam and the group of robed figures into the black night.

Chapter Twenty-One

Still crouching, we hid beside a tall pine tree, yards from the front door of the icehouse. A thin band of yellow light came from above and underneath the door. Otherwise, everything was dark. What was going on inside? Images flickered in my mind: the women lighting the black candles and waving their hands over the centerpiece of human hair, maybe reading from the books. Or worse. What if they were preparing for a sacrifice?

Even without windows, Liam and I might still be able to see something. Light spilled weakly from above the oversized door's frame, but there was no way to get up there. On the side of the building though was a gap where a single crooked board let out more light. I motioned to Liam to follow me. We ran, awkward and hunched over, toward the broken board.

Raindrops plopped hard on our jackets, rolling off the overhang above and hitting our shoulders as we pressed our faces close to the opening. Liam could see easily inside, but I was too short. Wedging the toes of my sneakers between the rocks of the foundation, I stood on tiptoes, barely at eye level.

It took a few seconds to get my bearings. At first, there were only shadows. Then movement. Shapes flickered in the yellow light, but they were disjointed. Like those puzzles where you can see only a portion of the picture: a hand holding a candlestick, the corner of a table, the railing to the back of an old chair. I stretched further and was rewarded with a wider view. The hooded figures stood around a table. In the center were the black candles and the hair I'd seen last time. One of the figures in a black robe held a pillar candle and swirled around the black ones in a slow circle. The first figure lit more pillar candles. Each figure held one and started the same slow circle around the items on the table. I squinted, tried harder to see who was there. If—

A woman screamed inside the building. I jerked. My feet slipped on the rock under me. Liam grabbed the shoulder of my jacket to stabilize me. I brought my face close to the opening. The shadowy shapes loomed, but it was hard to see them clearly through the small gap. The circles though, grew faster. The first set of hands bounced and swayed back and forth in chaotic and dizzying circles. It wove and bobbed as though the candle itself were moving and the hand was simply holding on. Rather than becoming weaker, the flame grew both in height and strength.

I stared at the flame that was now half as tall as the candle itself. There was a moan from somewhere in the room. Another sound, this one, deeper and shorter, more a grunting shout. It morphed into another noise: thick and hushed. It started as a low rumble and grew louder.

Words that I couldn't understand, twisted and thick sounding. Yet familiar somehow. They slid over and over one another. Like a low, old creaking. I closed my eyes, knowing these words. It was similar to what Venetia had said during our time together in her office. Except now, rather than filling me with warmth and a sense of peace, fear slid through my chest like a knife. The words grew louder, pulsating, a frenzied tone. They came faster and faster, keeping time with the hand that was still circling, circling.

I pushed forward, bumping my nose on the rough board. A small figure in a white robe was escorted to the table and shoved into a chair. She—I couldn't imagine a man that small— struggled against them. At that second, the white hood fell free.

It was Gwen.

At least I thought so. She looked drugged and her face was all wrong. In place of the pale, fine-boned features, her skin undulated in the shadows. Her eyes bulged then went back to normal, her chin and jawbones slid lower on her face and then back into position.

"What's happening to her?" Liam's voice was hoarse near my ear. "What are they doing? We need to—"

I grabbed his arm, fingers digging into his flesh. I couldn't look away from Gwen's face. It contorted, then went back to normal, then contorted again, as though another face sat just behind her own. I shuddered, unable to look away. Liam muttered something I didn't hear and shifted away from me. I tipped when he moved and grabbed the rough wooden boards to stay upright. I leaned into them and watched, equal parts horrified and fascinated.

"Tlaltecuhtli, great Mother of the Earth." I recognized Venetia's voice. "We raise this sister to you. Great Mother— who gives life and devours it—we come here in your presence with pure hearts. We acknowledge that you are a hungry spirit god, one whose needs are great. And yet you give us so much in return for our obedience to you. Mystical Mother, Tlaltecuhtli, your servant sisters bow before your greatness. You give us life, full harvests, you provide for us. In return, we offer you—"

The door of the icehouse burst open. Liam stood there, dripping rain, a branch raised in his hand.

No, Liam. No, no, no.

I turned to see better but my left foot slid off the rock. I fell to my knees in the mud below. At that same moment, the floorboards inside the icehouse rattled and the building vibrated. The women inside gasped. Someone cried out.

I grabbed for the edge of the icehouse, but a branch full of wet leaves got dislodged and slapped me in the face, making me sputter. Scrubbing at my eyes with the soggy arms of my jacket, I scrambled to my feet.

Inside, a chair screeched over the floorboards. Feet shuffled. There was another grunting yelp and then a heavy, dull thud. My breath came fast between my teeth. My legs wouldn't move.

Do something, my brain screamed at my body. *Anything.*

Finally, my feet found more solid footing. I eased myself back into the spot where Liam had stood seconds before and peered through the crack in the wall. The candles glowed cheerfully, inappropriate to the grim scene they illuminated.

"You fool," Venetia hissed. She walked toward Liam.

He was on his knees, doubled over. His head hung low. Paula lashed his hands together behind his back with a skinny gray rope. Liam moaned. His head lolled to the side, blood smeared across his forehead.

"Get him up," Venetia's voice was clear and commanding in the near quiet. The rain had nearly stopped. I felt dazed as Paula hauled Liam to his feet.

"Where?" She looked at Venetia.

"The barn," Venetia said. "Quickly. We don't have much

time." She glanced across the room, directly toward me. For a single, awful second, I thought I'd been discovered. But then she looked back toward Paula.

"Take Randi if you need help."

Randi stood up but Paula grunted a negative and hauled Liam along, whispering something in his ear. He slumped further in response and shuffled jerkily toward the door, tipping to one side. Paula kept a hand on his waistband. Clenched in her other hand was a hammer.

I looked back at the others. Gwen too, was bound. Her hands were placed carefully on the table in front of her. A rope had been wound around her wrists and a white-handled knife had been jammed through it, deep into the table underneath. Her face was bone white and hollow-eyed. Her eyes were vacant.

"We don't have much longer," Randi pulled up the sleeve of one coat sleeve daintily and looked at her watch. "It's nearly time."

Venetia frowned more deeply but said nothing.

"Idyll Weise was built on this ceremony," Randi continued. "If we don't make it before—"

"We will."

"Are you sure? And what about him?" Randi's voice had risen an octave. She waved her hand toward the open door. "What are we going to do with him?"

"Leave that to me. Paula will be back shortly. We'll finish the ceremony, and all will be as it should be."

"But—"

"All will be as it should be," Venetia repeated the words loudly and stared at Randi who looked back at her for several long seconds before lowering her gaze with a sigh.

The seconds ticked by.

Move, move, move!

But go where? Should I run after Paula and try to free Liam? Or wait here? Maybe I could help Gwen.

What were they going to do to her? Randi's words rolled around in my head. *We don't have much longer.*

Before what?

The rain had stopped and the moon, full and round under the smeary black clouds, shone brightly overhead. I wedged myself in closer to the building, hoping that Paula wouldn't see me when she returned.

My fingers, clenching the board, had gone numb and I realized I was shaking hard. I wondered vaguely about hypothermia as the door creaked loudly.

"It's done," Paula breathed heavily. "We'd better hurry."

Venetia nodded, her long, black robe swaying as she once again wove the tall taper candle around Gwen's head in circles. The chanting began again. Periodically I heard *Tlaltecuhtli.* A faint memory tugged at me. Where had I heard that before? Something to do with an ancient art history class I'd taken in college.

"Tlaltecuhtli, great Mother of the Earth . . ." the voices droned.

Mother. That word brought the slippery thought closer. I closed my eyes, seeing Dr. Cronkle with his little round glasses and always-rumpled beige suit. He used to stride back and forth across the front of the room, never still.

Tangled with the images was the word, Tlaltecuhtli. I could almost hear his German accent, and smell the mix of paper and dust motes in the classroom. Goddess. That was it. Tlaltecuhtli had been a goddess of the Incas. Or was it the Aztecs? I closed my eyes, seeing the slides Dr. Cronkle had projected. A hideously ugly sculpture of the woman god came rushing back. She'd been famous for something important to the people of the ancient world. Was it fertility? Love?

". . . and we offer up to you now, Earth Mother, this daughter of light. Let her be named, great Goddess of Earth. Goddess of life and death—"

I closed my eyes, tried to remember more about her.

"She was a hungry one, Tlaltecuhtli." My professor's voice echoed in my memory. "One of the goddesses who required human sacrifice." He'd clasped his hands together a little gleefully.

Human sacrifice.

I opened my eyes, clutching the board tighter.

Gwen. Were they going to—

"We crown this new sister tonight in your great name and offer her for your service."

If they were offering her for service, they wouldn't kill her. Right?

Unless being a sacrifice was her service.

I couldn't just stand here and watch. I looked around for something to use as a weapon.

A shuffling noise inside. I turned back.

Venetia held something over Gwen's head. My throat felt like it was sealed shut. I strained to get a better look as the chanting rose from the women again. Candlelight flickered and caught the blade of the white-handled knife. The one that had pinned the rope to the table was now positioned over Gwen's head.

Chapter Twenty-Two

A scream nearly escaped but caught on my teeth and died in a whimper. Venetia brought the sharp instrument closer to Gwen's head. The boards under my fingers bit hard into my skin.

Do something!

But I was immobilized. Transfixed by the scene before me.

The blade glinted in the light. Venetia brought it to Gwen's forehead and then in great, careful passes, she cut away all the long, tangled dreadlocks. The blade was so sharp the dreadlocks fell away like curls of butter. Gwen closed her eyes but other than that showed no sign of life. There was rustling in the undergrowth to the right of me. Distracted, I turned to see a fat opossum waddle out from the leaves and tangles of branches. It continued on its way, not pausing to look at me.

Liam. I needed to go and find him. Before they finished this—this ceremony. But if I did that, I'd leave Gwen all alone. Still, what good was I doing here?

Liam or Gwen? Liam or Gwen?

There had been blood on Liam's forehead. The cut might be deep, and he needed my help. And if he hadn't been able to save Gwen, how could I? Liam at least, must be unguarded.

". . . place of our dear sister, Ruby, we offer you this fresh vessel for service, oh great Mother, Tlaltecuhtli." Venetia's voice was harder to hear, as she bent over Gwen, cutting away the last of the dreadlocks. Gwen's head looked like a newborn's, perfectly round and horribly exposed.

"Stand." Venetia pushed Gwen's shoulders. But the younger woman remained slumped at the table, staring without seeing something across the room. Venetia motioned to Paula who slipped with surprising grace to Gwen's side. She lifted the younger woman to her feet, her ropy arms around her middle. Gwen stood, supported like a doll on a display stick, her arms dangling. Paula whispered something into her ear. Gwen blinked a few times and straightened her body, holding onto the table, her fingers gripping the edge hard.

Randi stood too, her black robe falling away at the neck. She regathered the fabric, looked from Gwen to Venetia and back again.

"Now?" she asked quietly.

Venetia nodded once. Randi pulled out a small book and cleared her throat.

"Hurry," Paula's voice was soft and urgent. "We don't have much time."

"Great Mother, Tlaltecuhtli," Randi began, swaying gently from side to side as she read. "We come before you and offer up this sister to your care . . ."

I didn't stay to hear the rest. My feet slipped over wet patches of leaves and mud sucked at my shoes as I tried to run. It seemed to take ages but was seconds, maybe a minute before I arrived at the barn. I fumbled with the latch. My nearly numb fingers slipped off again and again. Paula hadn't locked the door, thankfully. Finally, the latch creaked open in my hands.

I plunged into the darkness, not daring to use the flashlight. My breath was so loud I couldn't hear anything else. I forced myself to be quieter so I could hear other sounds in the large space.

"Liam?" My whisper was loud in the cavernous barn.

A groan came from the right. I shuffled in that direction, hands out in front of me. Moonlight fell sporadically through the barn's boards, slivers of light that bounced and then faded away as the rolling clouds got in the way. The equipment still crouched in the corners under tarps. The same mixture of old hay and dust, gasoline, and a rusty, metallic smell filled the air.

Another moan, this time closer.

Had it come from the lumpy shapes against the far wall? I headed toward them. My legs shook. A flutter of panic crawled up my esophagus.

Get out.

How long would it be before they came looking for Liam and whatever they had planned for him?

"Liam?"

There was rustling from under the tarp furthest away. I ran to it and yanked it back. Paint-chipped pieces of wood were stacked neatly. No sign of Liam.

"Wh . . . what happened?" His voice was groggy, coming from my right.

I jerked off another tarp. Liam lay on his side, legs, and arms pulled up close. He shivered uncontrollably. His hands were still bound with rope, his eyes bleary.

"We've got to get out of here. Can you walk?"

He nodded, then shook his head and moaned. "I think so . . . not sure."

"Come on, we need to hurry."

I positioned my shoulders under his left arm awkwardly because of the ropes. I wished I had a knife with me. His weight slid away immediately. I tried again but the same thing happened.

"Let's get these ropes off."

"There's a jackknife in my back pocket. It's . . . small but sh-should work."

I turned him enough so that I could fish the jackknife out. It was pearl-handled and so smooth it nearly slipped from my icy fingers.

"Here." I brought it to his hands. "Let me see." I struggled to get the thin blade out with my stiff fingers.

"I'm glad you came." His voice was sleepy.

Did he have a concussion?

"I tried . . . to get the knife but . . . I'm so tired."

I sawed away at the rope. It was surprisingly strong for being thin.

"Can you pull?" I showed Liam with my hands that I wanted him to maintain tension on the rope. He blinked his eyes open and stared at me for a full five seconds before nodding.

"Sure." His voice was slightly slurred. That wasn't good.

"Now." The pressure on the rope tightened slightly.

I continued sawing at the rope but glanced back over my shoulder every few seconds. I was sure that Venetia or one of the others would barge in and whack me over the head.

I gripped the knife's handle harder. It kept sliding in my damp hand. The rope had gone lax again. Rather than trying to get Liam to adjust the tension, I did it myself, pulling at the restraint with one hand and cutting at it with the other. Finally, there was a low popping sound. The rope twisted and frayed enough that I could work Liam's hands free.

I helped him to his feet next, keeping the knife blade extended away so I wouldn't stab him accidentally. We shuffled awkwardly for a minute like junior high kids at their first dance. Finally, his arm was over my shoulders.

"We're going to my car." My voice was low and urgent in the dead stillness of the barn. The last of the rain had stopped and even the big plops falling from branches overhead onto the metal roof had lessened significantly. Were my keys in the car? I pictured them dangling from the ignition, hoping I was right.

At least I could stow Liam there where it was dry and run back to the retreat house to look for my keys again. Or I might be able to do a rolling start. Driving an old car with a stick shift had its benefits.

"Let's go."

We stumbled and I grunted as Liam stepped on my foot then overcorrected, nearly throwing us off balance. By the time we'd reached the barn door though, we'd worked out a sort of herky-jerky motion that resembled walking. I poked my head through the open doorway, scanned the landscape. I could still see a faint yellow light trembling between the cracks of the icehouse. That was a good sign.

"Hurry," I urged Liam toward the woods and the little path that led away from the grounds. "My car is this way."

". . . going?" he asked and tripped over a branch. I gasped involuntarily and tried to right us but couldn't. We landed in the mud of the dirt path. Liam's head was inches from the thick trunk of a half-dead tree. I hurried to get us both up and keep moving.

They could be coming any minute.

They could be—

A branch broke behind us. I whirled around—or tried to— and nearly catapulted us into the mud again. I scanned the area but couldn't see anything.

"Racoon maybe." My voice sounded surprisingly confident, but my heart hammered hard against my ribs and my armpits felt damp. How far was the car now? It felt as though we were walking through quicksand. Liam moaned and his head lolled to one side.

"You okay?"

"No," he whispered back, his voice little more than a croak. "My head . . . issh." He stopped and tried again. "Issh kill . . . me."

In other circumstances, I might have laughed. Now, I only gritted my teeth and tried to keep him upright.

"It's not far," I panted, unsure if that was true. "We're nearly there."

Liam wasn't a small guy and his weight crushed me. I felt like an insect on one of those velvet-covered boards, pinned in place. My legs shook with effort to keep us standing.

Bare tree branches clicked together. It reminded me for some reason of a horror movie I'd seen with an old boyfriend in college. There were these spooky-looking grayish aliens with long talons that clicked together right before they fed. I shoved the thought away and counted steps, pausing every so often to rest and readjust Liam's sliding weight again.

Finally, we crested a little knoll. Beyond it was the rustic parking area. I saw my car. All the breath whooshed out of my lungs. Tears of relief blurred my view and I blinked them away. But what was that—no. Oh no.

A tree lay across the driveway, completely blocking the way out.

Chapter Twenty-Three

I swore under my breath. Liam blinked groggily and squinted, trying to focus on the scene.

" . . . wh . . . happened?"

"A tree fell," I snapped, instantly feeling bad. It wasn't his fault he was so helpless. Panic gathered in my chest though, hot and tight. I wanted to scream and throw my arms in the air and run away. I wanted someone else to figure this out. Mostly, I just wanted to go back to before I'd come here. Back home, in my little apartment, looking at the nasty weather outside my window as I sipped tea and pulled my sweater tighter, and thought how grateful I was that I didn't have to go anywhere.

That's not helping. Think, think!

I helped Liam to a tree, leaning him awkwardly against it in a sitting position, and told him I'd be right back. Swiping at my eyes, I straightened my aching shoulders and walked purposefully toward the car. Maybe I could move the tree. Or get the car out another way? Even as I thought about it, I knew how hopeless the situation was. The tree was as big around as a watermelon. I pushed and shoved at it anyway, desperation more than hope fueling my actions. The rough bark scraped against my burning palms.

This was stupid. A waste of time. And a rolling start was

out of the question since I needed to let the car *roll* to pick up enough speed.

Keys.

I'd forgotten to look for them. I scrambled around to the driver's door, searched every inch of the car frantically but found nothing.

No. No. No.

I leaned back against the tree's trunk, my heartbeat pounding rhythmically in my head. Hopelessness crashed over me like an ocean wave. The mud sucked at my shoes and the tree branches overhead kept clicking. We had to get out of here. Liam needed a doctor. Gwen needed . . . rescue. I was the only one of us who had a car here.

Think, Flora, think.

There had to be a way.And then an idea came, bubbled up like a little spring of fresh water. I'd seen another car, an old Volvo station wagon that Paula had used to bring eggs to town to sell the second morning. It must be how they'd picked everyone else up—the carpooling. The driveway was narrow and rutted but the old car had been impervious.

I looked back to assess the situation from a new angle. The tree had fallen neatly in the makeshift parking area, almost like it had been placed by a giant's hand. The top protruded into the driveway itself but I could avoid it. I thought I could anyway. My heart thudded hard in my chest, faster at the thought of it.

Escape.

But first, I had to find the keys. Pressing my fingers against my closed eyes, I searched the Retreat Center in my mind. Where had I seen the keys? The kitchen. Just inside the back door among the hooks of coats and sweaters and the tall cabinet topped with harvest baskets. I remembered the keys jingling when I'd cut through the doorway on my way to the pond.

A flutter of hope tickled my chest. First, though, I had to get Liam out of the cold and wet. He was slumped over on his side and didn't open his eyes when I shook his shoulder gently.

"Liam?"

No response.

"Liam, can you hear me?"

A soft groan.

"My head—"

"I know. We're going to the hospital. I need you to get into my car, okay? Can you do that?"

He blinked long, slow, sleepy blinks. ". . . yesshhh."

"Good."

I put my arms around him again and using the tree for support, got him to his feet. It took several long, uncomfortable minutes to get him to the car and a few more to fold him into the backseat. His tall frame filled most of it. I shook out a spare blanket from the emergency roadside kit my grandmother had given me for Christmas one year and tucked it tightly around him. It didn't cover him. He was too tall, but I made sure his core was wrapped up. He shivered nonstop and his eyes closed again. I couldn't remember much about concussions, only that you shouldn't let the person sleep. But what choice did I have? If I didn't get the other car and get us out of here, we'd be in even more danger.

I closed the car door quietly and ran back along the path we'd struggled up. It took only minutes for me to get back to the house. A single light glowed from an upstairs window, but the curtains were drawn. My gaze automatically went toward the icehouse, but I couldn't see it from where I stood.

I ran along the house's length and entered through the kitchen door. Or tried to. It was locked. I groaned and retraced my steps. None of the doors in the house were ever locked. Maybe something had fallen, blocking it from the inside?

My shoes squished on the front steps, leaving tracks of mud. I tried to quiet my breathing as I pushed the door open. I half-expected to find Venetia, Randi, and Paula there with angry accusing faces, their hands outstretched, ready to grab me.

The hallway was empty. A single lantern burned low on a squat table at the end of it. I walked as quietly as I could toward the kitchen, hoping none of the boards underfoot squeaked.

The dining room was covered in shadows. I maneuvered through tables, banged my shin on one of the hard-backed chairs, and groped with my hands outstretched until I reached the kitchen. It too was dark, smelling faintly of the berry muffins that had been served for breakfast and of something herby and earthy.

I crossed quickly to the wall by the back door. Three hooks were planted there, amidst the jumble of jackets and sweaters, just like I remembered. One hook held the ring of keys. I said a silent prayer of thanks and grabbed them. I forced myself to take a couple of deep breaths as I moved to the back door.

The cabinet to the right of the door had shifted slightly to the left, blocking the doorframe just enough to keep it from opening. Had someone pushed it there purposefully? I shoved against the tall wood cabinet, but it might as well have been made of concrete.

A noise behind me.

I stopped.

Something in the hallway.

A creak of a floorboard. A footstep?

I swallowed; my throat dry. Moving back into the dining room, I pressed my back against the wall. My hands groped in the darkness. Skirting tables and chairs, I crouched by the banquet. Hidden in the shadows, I waited.

Nothing. Only the *tick, tick, tick* of the old and ugly wooden clock on the far wall. I squinted, tried to see the time but couldn't.

I stayed where I was for a few more long minutes, my thighs burning. Finally, I stood. The room was empty. A breath trembled from my mouth in a shaky exhale. Carefully and painstakingly slowly, I made my way toward the door to the hallway. *No one was there. No one.* I repeated it like a mantra.

Nearly there. Just a few more steps. I poked my head out, looking to the right. Nothing. I turned to the left.

A shadowy form stood less than a foot from me. Stifling a gasp, I ducked back into the dining room. My heart slammed against my ribs. Whoever it was must have been looking the other way. Would she come in here next? See me? I ducked back beside the banquet, grateful for its hulking shape.

Several agonizingly long seconds passed before the figure crossed into the dining room and continued their way into the kitchen. I waited longer, not daring to move in case I bumped into something or made a floorboard squeak.

Quiet.

Then a heavy sigh. Something metal rattled against something else and there was an unintelligible mumble. The figure reappeared at the door and leaned against it.

Finally, after what felt like an hour, the figure retraced his or her steps back across the dining room, seeming to have no trouble seeing where they were going. I waited several more minutes before standing and crossing to the doorway. Sharp pricks of pain ran up my legs as blood rushed back into them. I hesitated, lingering by the edge of the doorframe.

Were they gone? Or waiting for me?

I poked my head out and looked to the right and left. No one was there. I slipped down the hallway, careful to stay nearer the wall where the boards weren't as likely to squeak.

I was nearly to the front door. A dim, cold light shone through the side glass panels. My heart picked up pace again as I thought through my next steps. The car was parked in a makeshift carport attached to the back of the house. I'd get in, lock the doors, drive to Liam, then get to the nearest town with a phone and call for an ambulance—

A hand fell on my shoulder.

My heart stopped.

"Where do you think you're going?" a voice asked from the shadows.

Chapter Twenty-Four

I jumped, let out a muffled cry.

The figure stepped forward from the shadows.

"I'll take the keys." Paula held out her hand, the other one dug into my shoulder, nails burrowing into flesh.

Inexplicably, a fragment of a sentence floated into my mind. *And if you think you can't, the battle is already lost. But if you think of the possibilities. . .* A motivational speaker on the public TV station Nona had loved.

The car was only a few precious yards away. Just out the door and around the back of the house. I let my shoulders sag. Defeated, I fumbled with the keys.

"The ring is stuck on my finger."

As Paula leaned in closer with her bulldog face for a better look, I jerked my elbow upward hard. It connected with her nose. There was a stomach-churning crunch. Blood spurted. She cried out, her hands instinctively flying to her face. I sprinted out the door and toward the back where the carport was.

Was she coming after me? Any second, I expected to feel her claw-like grip on my shoulders again. I ran faster. My feet slid in some wet leaves, and I nearly fell, catching myself at the last second on the car's hood.

Jumping inside, I jammed the key into the ignition. Gave it gas. Without bothering with the lights I rammed the old Volvo into gear. It shot out of the structure. I switched too hard into second, the gears ground together. Something under the hood whined. I jabbed the shifter back into first and flicked on the lights.

The woods along the drive were shadowy and dark. Branches leaned over it as though reaching for me. I glanced in the side mirror. A dark figure ran after me.

I screamed, the sound shrill in the enclosed space.

How had Paula managed to get this far already? Wildly, I checked the mirror again. She yelled something but I didn't stop to find out what.

The driveway was little more than a muddy cow path and the car veered and jerked as it sped over lumps and ruts. It jittered into and out of potholes. I hit one so hard that my teeth snapped together. I whimpered, a panicky fear squeezing my chest, but kept my foot pressed hard on the accelerator.

Close now. I was seconds away from my car and Liam. I'd get Liam out of my car. Both of us into the Volvo. Drive to town and find a phone. Would I remember the way back? I didn't have a map this time and Liam wouldn't be much help.

I slowed slightly as I crested the little knoll close to the parking area. My car crouched there, hemmed in by the fallen tree. I got the Volvo as close as I could to my car without being in the path of the tree and slammed on the brakes. How much time did we have? Maneuvering Liam out of the backseat with Paula so close behind would be tricky. Still, I'd driven a good two minutes, hadn't I? She couldn't run that fast.

I hustled to my car and jerked open the door.

The backseat was empty. I stood, panting, felt a single drop of sweat track down my backbone. Shivering, I scanned the area. *Where are you?* He must have woken up, confused, and staggered off. I circled the car, even ducked and peeked underneath. Nothing. I made a wider circle.

"Liam," I whispered hoarsely. "Liam, where are you?"

I made the circles wider and wider but there was still no sign of him. I forced myself to keep searching. But every second put me at greater risk. Paula or someone else would be here soon, take the car, our one chance of escape.

But I couldn't leave him out here. Liam could die of exposure or wild animals or . . . who knew what else? He had to be here somewhere. But where?

"Liam?"

There was a noise in the bushes just beyond where I was standing. I stood still and listened. Seconds later, it sounded again. A dull moan. Or had it been tree branches, rubbing together overhead? I headed that way, covering the uneven ground as fast as possible.

There it was again. It was louder and definitely human.

I ran toward the general area it had come from, gasping when I saw Liam, laying in the mud near a small pine tree. His head rolled toward me as I drew closer. His eyes were glazed and unfocused. His chest jerked sporadically.

Rushing to his side, I touched his face. It was icy under my hands.

"What are you doing out here?" I scolded, but then when he didn't answer, tried to roll him onto his back. "It's all right. I have a car. We can—"

"No need," a voice said from behind me.

My breath stuttered in my throat.

"We'll take care of you both back at the house."

When I turned it felt like it was in slow motion. I didn't want to see the face that belonged to the voice. In some stupid, childish way I believed that if I didn't see it, it would go away and this whole nightmare would end. I'd be back home in bed, blankets wrapped around me, a pillow beneath my head. I'd wake up to another normal, deliciously mundane day.

But the thought evaporated quickly. Four people stood close by. Paula and Randi with Gwen wedged between them.

And closer to me, Venetia, her face twisted with anger.

"You should have minded your own business, girl."

I saw something in her hand—heavy and dark. I put my hands up instinctively. An explosion of bright blue pain arced across my head.

And then everything went black.

Chapter Twenty-Five

I woke, a dull roar like a waterfall ran through my head. I blinked slowly but the darkness didn't subside. Turning my head caused a moan to slip from between my teeth, a deep, pain-filled noise. My head throbbed and I closed my eyes again.

Then I remembered Venetia and the others. The woods. I'd tried to run. Something incredibly solid had been whacked against the side of my head. A branch or someone's walking stick. I tried to move my eyebrows and something tacky cracked open.

Two hits to the head in less than two days. Did I have a concussion now, like Liam?

Liam.

Where was he? I tried to say his name but all that came out was a moan that started with an "L" sound. I forced my eyes open, blinked against the darkness.

Where *was I?* Behind the roar in my ears was another sound. A clang, then some ticking. I moved my arms and gently explored my face and head with fingers that felt swollen and cold. I was shivering, I realized, with a detachment that made an arrow of fear zing in my chest. Hypothermia. I needed to move.

Stand up, figure out where you are. Find Liam.

But everything was so hard. My legs, like my arms, felt weighted and cold, like the big blocks of ice that must have once been stored in the icehouse. Could that be where I was? The clang sounded again and then continued clicking. I'd heard it somewhere recently. The answer flitted just out of reach in my brain.

Pushing my block-like arms under me, I lifted my upper torso off the ground. The floor was dirt but there was a feeling of walls around me, not open space like the outdoors. And it was musty.

The basement.

Having that small piece of information felt good, and centered me. I drew another breath, prepared to struggle to my feet. The sounds—the clang and the clicks—were from when I'd followed Blue down here.

Blue.

I wished he were here now. Remembered his words: "We hear some strange things about these women and this house . . . tales that make the skin crawl."

I'd been stupid. Had let my curiosity get the better of me without putting any sort of precautions in place.

If I'd left before, when Gwen approached me, I'd be home now. Or if I'd taken off right after George and I explored the icehouse, would the leaders of Idyll Weiss be sitting in jail cells? Or if I hadn't come here, to begin with . . .

But I hadn't trusted my gut. I hadn't taken any of it seriously. I'd been suspicious. But not enough to make a difference. Not until the ceremony.

Where was Liam? I slouched heavily against the basement wall. It was made of fieldstones and felt warm after the earthen floor, which was cold and damp.

I had to find him. Get us both out of here. Or go on my own and get help if I couldn't. My body ached like the very worst flu I'd ever had. The worst of the pain though, was my skull. I reached up and gingerly felt the right side where the pain radiated in waves. I felt a crust of dried blood and a gash that was still tacky.

I swallowed, squinted into the darkness again. I had to get my bearings. How had I gotten down here? The last thing I remembered hazily, were the women in the forest, the car tantalizingly close but so far away, and Liam, his face blocked out by one of the figures standing above him like a dark, menacing shadow.

Had they killed him?

The shivering was uncontrollable and it wasn't only from the temperature. Fear darted through me like a hummingbird, flitting here, there, and everywhere.

I forced myself to take a couple of deep breaths, spoke firmly to myself through chapped, dry lips.

"Calm down. You're no good to anyone if you're hysterical. You've got to figure this out. Just think about the first step. Don't worry about everything after that."

The sound of my voice in the blackness soothed me. It also got me moving. I took a first hesitant step then another and another. Keeping my hands on the rough stone wall, I blocked out thoughts about rats and spiders and other things that like dark, musty old basements. Instead, I inhaled with every other step, slow and measured, and tried to ignore the jackhammer in my head.

"Good, you're doing good."

For a second, I had a strange out-of-body type feeling. Was I really here? Was all of this real?

"Keep going," my whispered voice encouraged. "Another step. Good—"

My foot hit something soft but firm. I froze. It could be anything. A bunch of old clothes wrapped up tightly. An old doll. A bag of flour.

Please, please let it be one of those things.

I sank to my knees and whimpered. Hands out in front of me, I patted blindly at the air near the floor. I felt nothing at first, just emptiness.

But then my left palm struck something solid and fabric-covered. I brought my right close to it, hesitated, then felt it with both hands.

Fabric. Some torn. A button was undone.

Beneath it lay a body, hard and cold.

Chapter Twenty-Six

I couldn't hold in the scream, though I did manage to clamp a hand over my mouth which drowned out most of it. I felt through my pockets. *Stupid, stupid!* Why hadn't I thought to check for my cell phone before this? My hand closed around the scratched case. I pulled it out, fumbled in the darkness, and jabbed my finger in the approximate area of the flashlight but nothing happened. I poked at the screen again and again. I swallowed down a dull panicky whine. The light flicked on finally, blinding me in a wash of bright light. Blue squiggles danced and wound themselves around in front of me. I blinked several times and pointed the light at the body on the floor.

It was Liam. He lay straight and rigid on his side.

Was he—

I shuddered and pulled on his shoulder. He rolled onto his back stiffly. His eyes, open but vacant, stared at the ceiling. A gasping sob erupted from my throat. I didn't bother trying to smother it this time. I scooted away from his body instinctively, all the way back until I hit the other wall. Then I drew my knees to my chest, panting.

This couldn't be real. *Wake up!* I commanded myself. *Wake up. You're dreaming. This isn't happening.*

But it *was* really happening. I was here, in the basement of a God-forsaken house in the middle of nowhere. And crazy women were trying to kill us. They had killed Liam. I sucked in a breath. My airway felt as narrow as a stir stick.

Soon, I might be dead down here too, staring frozenly like Liam. I imagined some long-lost cousin being called into some official office years from now, a fragment of my hair or bone or other DNA sample extracted from my withered corpse. Warm tears mixed with the dried blood on my face, making it itch. In the middle of a sob, I wiped a hand over my cheeks, then rubbed the mess onto my shirt. I hauled myself to my feet again, breath shaky between cold lips. My knees shook, my ribs felt pinched and sore, and my head throbbed harder than ever.

There had to be a way out of here. And I needed to find it. Before they came back. They would come back, a panicky squeeze filled my chest. Of course, they would. They couldn't leave Liam down here forever. Me, either. What were they planning to do with me? My mind was filled with images of Aztecs and other early tribes—ritual killings, human sacrifices. I saw myself being hauled up to the top of a burning pyre, or tangled in ropes with rocks in my pockets and tossed into the nearby pond, or maybe they'd—

Stop it.

Focus on getting out of here, not letting panic run wild. If I panicked, I was dead.

"Dead," I said the word out loud. Unlike earlier, it didn't bring me comfort. But it did help break the cycle of my spinning thoughts.

I cleared my throat and tried again. "Think clearly. Be rational."

That was better.

My heart rate slowed a millisecond.

"The first thing to do is get out of the basement," I said, my voice just a tiny bit calmer.

Maybe there was another door, one that led directly outside. Lots of old basements had hatchways—places where firewood was dumped in, or in the old days, coal would have been. Or a window somewhere. The chances of the basement not having another exit were slim. I just had to find it. And then, once I was out of the house, I'd run through the woods if I had to, and find the main road. Or hide in the forest until the emergency crews came.

Moving in the opposite direction of Liam's body, I shone the light around the low-ceilinged cellar. We were somewhere close to the stairs leading up to the first floor. That was where I'd followed Blue down to pester him with questions. The stairs were tempting but I doubted I'd have any luck getting out of the door above. It would be locked or otherwise blocked off. Or Venetia or one of the others might be guarding it.

I blinked and shone my light along the rough stone walls. There had to be another way out. I adjusted the screen, saw the battery. It was at thirteen percent. *Hurry, hurry.* I felt my way along the wall. The stones were rough and gritty with dirt under my fingertips. The light wobbled, and my arms shook uncontrollably.

Something skittered near my right foot. I jumped, bashing my elbow into the wall. Pain radiated up. Whatever it was had moved too quickly for me to see what it was. A black rat with a long, slimy tail and yellowed teeth? I pushed the thought away and picked up my pace.

This part of the basement was long and narrow enough that I could see both sides of it with the beam from my light. But the cellar extended further, moved out into a larger rectangle big enough so that I couldn't see the other side anymore. It was surprisingly neat and nearly empty. There were a few wooden crates stacked here and there, marked on the outside with black marker: "winter storage," and "off-season tools." I nearly walked by that one before stopping.

I fumbled with the wooden lid, tried to pry it up with my fingers, which slid right off. I needed something sturdy that I could use to leverage the lid up. I shone my light around, hoping it might show a crowbar or ax leaning conveniently in the corner. But there was nothing. Of course, if I'd found one of those, I wouldn't need to open the crate.

I continued walking, shone my light around corners and crevices. Every few feet I expected to find a dead end, but the basement went on and on. It felt like one of those amusement park rides that are pitch black—you feel like you're on the ride for hours instead of minutes, waiting for the next explosion or drop or animatronic to jump out at you.

My phone slipped through my stiff fingers as I stumbled over something and dropped to the dirt floor. I crouched and patted the ground until I found it again. I shone the light back the way I'd come. My heart stuttered in my chest.

Rounded and whitish gray, the thing shone pale and ghostly in the artificial light. It was . . . No, it couldn't be. I closed my eyes but when I opened them again, the small gravestone was still there. I hesitated, then moved toward it, running my fingers lightly over its surface. There were words here— probably a name and date—but I couldn't make them out. The surface was nearly smooth. It must be very old.

Swallowing hard, I sank back on my heels. My mind scrambled to process this new piece of horrifying information.

Why was there a grave in the basement?

Then I blinked, turned my head. Were there others? A whole cemetery down here? A bubble of hysteria rose in my chest, but I forced myself to breathe slow, regular breaths. I shone the light around.

There was another one, about four feet from where I stood, a tiny stone that rose only three or four inches from the floor. I hurried to it but again, couldn't make out the words. A thin layer of black mold covered most of its surface. And beyond that . . . I swallowed hard. Another stone sat about a yard or so away; that one like the second was small and lay horizontally. I'd nearly reached the opposite wall now.

Three. Three stones, lined up like windows in a house.

Wait. Not three. A fourth one was placed further away and on its own. Four bodies were buried in the basement. Shivers coursed through my system. I put a hand over my mouth to hold in the cry of alarm. It wasn't an uncommon practice. In the old days, death was very much a natural part of life. Before funeral homes and mortuary practices, the dead had been left in the home where wakes had taken place. The bodies would lay in the front room where they were watched over by their loved ones until the deceased was deposited into the family plot. Sometimes these were at the local churchyard. Other times, they were on the family's land. Small family cemeteries are certainly not unusual in rural parts of New England.

But the basement? Less usual, but not outside the realm of possibility. There had been a newspaper story about a couple who'd bought an old New England farmhouse sight unseen, intending to demolish it and build a new place over it. They'd been shocked to discover a tombstone in the basement. It turned out to be one of the farmhands. And the State had forbidden anyone to disturb the grave until his next of kin was tracked down. Other stories too, popped up in the news from time to time. I vaguely remembered one in southern Vermont. A family had lost more than one child to scarlet fever. They'd buried them neatly together like cordwood in an earthen-floor basement like this one.

Remembering this calmed me. The need to scream had died away and my heart wasn't jackhammering away in my chest anymore. I breathed deeply and moved past the makeshift graveyard, but a question circled repeatedly: who were they?

When I got out of here, I would research it, I promised myself. As I picked my way across a particularly rutted area of earth, I stumbled and caught myself on a crate. This one wasn't covered and with a dull thud, it fell over and spilled its contents over my feet. Something glinted in the light and I squatted and pulled an ancient-looking ax from the tangle of old, moldering rope, rusted metal canisters, and other odds and ends too decrepit looking to identify.

Hope fluttered weakly in my chest as I grabbed the splintery handle. I could use the ax to open the tool crate. Maybe there were more tools or even makeshift weapons. I'd use them to get out of here.

Backtracking quickly, I slipped by the desolate graveyard and found the crate again. It took only a few hits at the wooden sides with the pathetic ax before the fragile wood began to split away. The ax head bobbled on the end of the splintery handle. I worried it would soar completely off and hit me, but it clung on, sturdier than it looked. A stab of pain in my right palm. I gasped and jerked my hand away. Blood ran down my palm, but I ignored it and tore through the last of the disintegrating wood with my fingers. The contents of the crate fell out.

Chapter Twenty-Seven

Clothes. A patent leather purse in a horrible shade of yellow. A string of red plastic beads. A big yellow button with a smiley face. A set of car keys that had rusted. I grabbed the purse and opened it. Inside was a half-used lipstick in a rusted tube, a moldering handkerchief, and a carved leather wallet. I tried to open it but my fingers shook so hard it fell on the floor. I picked it up and unlatched the clasp. There was damp money in the back and a student ID card for someone named Jennifer Landry. The photo was faded but it was obvious the woman had been a college student back in the seventies. Her long hair and Peter Pan collar gave it away.

Blue. His story about the missing woman—the girl, he'd called her—rushed back. Was this her? Jennnifer Landry. Was she—instinctively, I looked behind me toward the gravestones. No, that would be stupid. If she'd died here she wouldn't be buried in a marked grave. A scuttling sound came from somewhere behind me. Little clawed feet moved along the stone walls.

The same bubble of panicky fear rose in my chest again, threatening to explode. I was stuck in a choose-your-own-ending story. Only all the endings were bad. Liam was dead. Gwen was brainwashed or drugged. My car was useless. I was trapped. How had our absences been explained to George and Imani? Where *were* they?

A noise sounded from back the way I'd come. A long, low creak. Something sliding against something else. A door opening? A floorboard outside of it? I wished I could hear better but the throbbing in my head was accompanied by a dull whooshing sound, like a swollen river. Whatever the noise was—whoever it was—I couldn't just sit here and let them find me. I slid the wallet into my back pocket and grabbed the ancient ax.

Flashing the light ahead of me I jogged back the way I'd come. The light bounced and wove, making shadows and shapes that jittered and danced on the walls.

Finally, I reached the end of the long basement. It came to a "T" and again, I thought of the reader-gets-to-choose books. *Flora comes to a junction. Should she go left or right? If right, turn to page—*

The sound came again. It was far behind me.

Footsteps.

Coming down the stairs.

One. Two. Three. *Pause.* Four, five—

Choose. Choose something.

I veered left, instinct telling me this was the way out. My breath rattled in the stone-lined space. The large basement had become narrow and cramped. What if I'd chosen the wrong way? What if this—

Something large and soft engulfed me. I screamed but it was muffled in the fur of whatever it was—a bear? coyote? mountain lion?—and I dropped my cell phone. Instant darkness. I jerked away, expecting the giant thing to come after me, to feel its claws slice through my skin. My arms and hands rose in front of my face. Nothing happened.

I waited for five seconds, ten.

Nothing. Kneeling, I scrabbled my hands around the moist earthen floor. Where was the light? My fingers groped over empty dirt. Finally, my left hand closed over the phone.

Immediately, I shone it upward. A very old-looking sheepskin was draped over something large and tall. I shone the light closer, getting to my haunches. Then, finally, I stood and put a shaky hand out toward it. The sheepskin fell away with a few hard tugs, revealing a pile of crates stacked from floor to ceiling. My heart sank. My teeth chattered uncontrollably.

It was a dead end.

I'd chosen the wrong way.

Chapter Twenty-Eight

I had to go back. Take the righthand turn instead.

But the sound of a voice, muffled through the gloom of the basement, reached me. "I know you're down here, Flora. This isn't a good place for you to be. I told her that. She doesn't listen though. She never listens . . ." The discombobulated voice dropped away.

About to turn back, I saw a faint glimmer of light past the stack of crates. What was it? I got closer and tried to steady the wobbling beam of light in my hand.

A crack of daylight. Barely coming in—maybe through the root cellar door or a hatchway—but it was definitely there. A beautiful strip of dove gray light. I scrambled up, tried to make my way over the crates, but they were too tightly pressed together. I couldn't get a foothold, couldn't grapple my way over the top. The sharp edges bit into my palms and I nearly lost my hold on the phone again.

I jumped back down. Heard the voice further back in the tunnel hit something and then curse as she stumbled. Or hopefully fell.

Heart pounding, I wedged my phone into the waistband of my pants, tossed the ax to the floor, and used both hands to pull at the crate closest to me. It moved a few inches but was heavy—far heavier than I'd expected.

Ignoring the panic that fluttered in my chest like a trapped bird, I pulled again and again. Finally, with a creak, the crate came free halfway. I picked up the ax and levered it in behind the rest of the crate. With a loud crack, the wooden box tumbled down onto the floor behind me. I heard glass break and turned. Jars of canned tomatoes exploded on the floor. The juice ran in rivers like blood onto the earth beneath.

The next crate came out a little easier. It was like playing a game of oversized Jenga, trying to pry the crates out of their places. Only now I didn't care if they all fell. I hoped they would. The voice behind me called out. I couldn't hear the words, but it sounded alarmed, maybe shouting a warning.

I smiled as another crate smashed to the floor, then a third.

Finally, the top tier wiggled.

"Stop!" the voice yelled. It was closer.

Footsteps pounded heavily over the ground. I held onto the ax and put all my strength into chopping at the uppermost level of the crates. At first, they only wobbled. But then one slid. And then another came free, banging and crashing down to the ground. I jumped back and barely missed being knocked off my feet by the one closest to me. There was a horribly loud crash, and more glass shattered.

I didn't bother stopping to look back this time. Just plunged upward, scrambled over the last of the crates and beyond to where the light was. With the ax out in front of me, I charged forward. Pain radiated in my shins as they hit something heavy and hard. I gasped, cried out, and fell forward, my hands skinned against the rough wood under them.

I patted the surface. Stairs. Beautiful, wonderful stairs leading up to the hatchway. I clambered up them, half crawling, and reached the top. I shined the light from my phone. There was a latch here, like a rusted peg. I gripped it and pulled it toward me.

It didn't move.

Shards of fear dug at my chest. I was suddenly lightheaded. The person—Randi it sounded like—was so close. Just on the other side of the crates.

"Flora, stop. I just want to—"

There was a yelp of pain. "I cut myself," her voice was incredulous. Then, "Flora—"

I'd been wrong. The latch didn't pull or push, it slid horizontally across the metal hatch door. I shoved it hard. The rusted thing creaked and groaned then slid neatly out of the way.

I pushed the heavy door up and out and climbed into the very cold, very early morning air.

Chapter Twenty-Nine

The heavy, hatch door slammed shut behind me. If only there was something heavy to push over it. Keep Randi trapped. She'd have to retrace her steps through the entire basement, which would buy me more time. There was nothing nearby though.

The woods behind the center were a dark gray smudge across an open field. I ran toward them. The open earth between me and it was pocked and pitted, a working field, I realized as I leaped at the last second over a divot that would have twisted my ankle or worse. My breath was ragged in my throat, which burned with dryness. I imagined people behind me, figures in dark cloaks running with weapons raised. But I didn't look back. Not until I reached the woods and slipped between the trees, panting, gasping. I leaned against a huge oak, letting it support me as I balanced on shaky legs.

I looked back across the field I'd just crossed. I waited for my eyes to adjust, to see torches raised. Hear the cackle of witches. See the scythes and pitchforks.

But there was nothing.

The field was still and silent, a gloomy mist hung over it like a curtain between this place and the house and outbuildings beyond. Where was Randi? Still trying to clamber over the boxes and crates? Had she realized I'd gotten out and gone to notify the others? Were they planning right now how to find me, drag me back?

In the macabre basement, my only thought had been to get out. But now what? Everything was working so slowly. I shook my head, clearing away the thoughts that hung like sticky cobwebbed strands in my brain. They'd come after me. And soon. They had to. There was too much at stake for them to just let me run.

I had to get to the road. Find help. Put as much distance between me and them as I could, as fast as I could. I'd stick to the trees. Use the woods for camouflage. Stay near enough to the property that I could follow the driveway. But stay deep enough in the woods not to be seen.

The thought of it all—the hundreds or thousands of steps ahead of me in the cold, gloomy air—made me want to sit down and rest my pounding head. But there was no time. Instead, I pulled my light jacket more tightly around me and started running in the direction of my car. The heat from exertion would keep me warm at least, keep me from slipping into hypothermia.

I hoped.

The forest was surprisingly noisy in the early dawn. Every bird in the area was chattering, screeching, or yammering about something. Staking claims, announcing what they were having for breakfast—who knew what birds discussed in the dull gray light of morning?

The terrain was rough, and I quickly slowed from a jog to a walk. I picked my way through downed branches and rotting tree trunks and skirted puddles. The puddles were beginning to freeze, the edges white and glittering. I thought longingly of my car—so close, yet so useless. Unless—

The ax. I'd forgotten about the ax that dug into my back uncomfortably. I'd shoved it in the waistband of my pants after hacking my way through the crates. I couldn't chop the tree— it was too big. But maybe I could hack down the bush that blocked the front of the car. At least cut off enough branches to get by it.

My feet picked up speed and a smile slipped onto my face. Could it work? Maybe. Maybe I could drive out of here, put miles between me and Idyll Weiss faster than I'd imagined. The thought made my chest feel as though it were filled with champagne.

Minutes later, I stood by my car, gasping. My head felt swollen like I was a huge Q-tip, my pulse threatened to explode my skull. I put a hand on the car. I wanted very much to hug it.

Detritus covered it. Branches and leaves were strewn everywhere like a tornado or hurricane had whipped through during the night. I was used to Vermont storms but this one had left more destruction than I'd ever seen before.

I ached to climb inside, lock the doors, rest. Instead, I pulled the ax free and walked to the front of the car. The bush that I'd parked behind was large—a lilac tree, I thought—and mature. A wave of disappointment crashed over me. The bush had thick, gnarled branches and a sturdy trunk.

There was no time to think about it. I swung the ax.

Thunk.

The blade made a small dent. My hands vibrated uncomfortably on the handle. I readjusted them and tried again. But again, the blade did little more than scuff the surface. I put my hand there, felt the wood. It was icy under my chilled fingers.

Maybe it had already frozen. It was out here, exposed to the cold air and wind. But it hadn't even snowed yet, more than a few anemic flakes. If only the blade was sharpened. I grimaced, pulled the ax behind me again, and let the weight of it drive my shaking arms forward.

Thunk. Thunk. Thunk.

Sweat formed in a film on my forehead. The ax finally bit into the wood of the trunk. I hit it again and again, not stopping for a rest. Afraid that if I did, I wouldn't be able to start again. My side screamed, begging me to rest. Instead, I swung and swung, as hard as I could with each pass, then harder still, until my arms wouldn't move anymore.

The lilac bush was tilted at an angle now, its trunk scarred and jagged. There was another quarter or so of the trunk to get through, but I couldn't move. I sat on the hood, breathing raggedly. Sweat ran in rivulets down my face. I smelled myself when I rubbed my arm over my forehead.

Squinting at the lilac bush, an idea formed. I used the ax to balance myself as I stood on the tree's trunk. My arms were spent but maybe I could break the rest of the trunk off using my bodyweight. I bounced, steadying myself with the ax handle.

Nothing.

I bounced again, harder. Then again and again.

A shout in the distance. From the direction of the Retreat Center.

I refocused on the trunk, jumped harder. It held though, and I wobbled like a beginning paddleboarder, struggling to maintain balance. But then with a crack, the last of the trunk broke free. I slipped, not ready for the upset, and fell to the ground, catching myself at the last second on the ax before I toppled into the mud underneath the bush. With the last of the strength in my arms, I pulled the bush to the side, clearing a way for the car.

I wanted to whoop in victory and do a little dance to celebrate. Instead, I slid my exhausted body into the driver's seat, closed the door, and laid my head against the wheel. My breath came out in little white puffs.

Would this work? I hadn't attempted a hill start since I was a teenager, sneaking out of my driveway to pick up my friends long after dark. Thank you, Uncle Freddy. The man hadn't paid much attention to me as a kid, but he had taught me some useful things as a teen.

Luckily, the ground here was steep, both behind and in front of the car. Unluckily, there was precious little room to let the car roll forward before it would run into a line of trees. The little path I'd followed to get to the house was far too small for even my little Ford.

If only I had the keys. If only I wasn't hurting so much, so tired. If only—

A deafening crack split the air. I jerked upright.

Was that a gun? Had they finally found me?

But then I saw a huge tree limb fall from a huge oak maybe twenty yards from the car. I watched as it tumbled from the other branches that must have been holding it up. It hit the ground and smashed. Bark and smaller branches flew off it like a detonated bomb. My palms were moist with sweat. I had walked under it ten minutes before. I would've been killed instantly if it had fallen on me. But it hadn't. Instead, it had dropped on the path leading to the Retreat Center. Blocking it.

I smiled and turned my attention back to the car. Fishing in the glovebox, I brought out the little, multipurpose jackknife.

It took several seconds of fumbling to find the small flat-head screwdriver. I pressed my tongue between my teeth and eased the screwdriver into the ignition. Then I clicked it to the *on* position.

Putting the car's shifter into neutral, I kept my left foot jammed on the clutch and my right planted on the brake. I'd only have one shot at this. If I missed it, the car would roll into the trees and I'd be just as stuck as before. I licked my lips, pressed them together, said a silent prayer, and held my breath.

As soon as the car started rolling, I lifted my foot from the clutch slowly. There was a loud, ugly-sounding scrape as the underside of the car cleared what was left of the lilac bush stump.

At first, that was the only noise there was. No sound of the engine turning over.

Come on. Come on!

Then the car coughed quietly. The trees were getting closer. I forced myself to go slow, not to make a mistake. I shoved the gearshift into first and gave it some gas. The car sputtered. The engine still didn't catch.

The trees were even closer now, the bark easy to see in the pearl-gray light. I squeezed my hands tight on the wheel and gave it more gas. Finally, the engine caught, and the car coughed to life. The windshield wipers squeaked against the dry glass, startling me. I jammed the clutch back in and applied the brake. The car's front bumper stopped in the undergrowth, inches from a big pine tree.

I let out a shaky squeal of pure joy. Finally, I was getting out of here.

Chapter Thirty

Carefully and very slowly, I put the car into reverse, completing an ugly three-point turn. First gear again. This time, I punched the gas a little harder to get up the small hill, an alternate way to the main drive. The knoll was covered in milkweed stalks. Small branches and bunches of leaves from the storm that had littered it. The grass was tall here and whispered along the sides of the car. I prayed there weren't any huge branches under all that grass, waiting to snag the undercarriage and moor it. The car jolted over dips and ruts in the earth, once dipping so low an ominous crunch sounded. I inhaled sharply, but the car scrambled over whatever lay there and further up the knoll.

Finally, the tires crunched onto the driveway. A bubble of laughter erupted from my throat. I glanced in the rearview mirror, checking again to see if anyone was following me, and nearly screamed. A wild woman stared back at me. My dark hair was matted and sticky with dark blood on one side. My face was streaked with dirt and grime. There was a big bruise around my jaw and cobwebs were stuck in my hair. Despite all of that though, I was smiling. Maniacally maybe but still. I looked back to the driveway.

Debris lay over most of it and some of the branches were too big to go over. I jumped out, dragged one especially large branch to the side, and climbed back in, holding my side. Seconds later, I had to repeat the process.

As I returned to the car, there was movement in the corner of my eye. The mirror on the passenger's side hung limply like a dead fish on a line of wires and black plastic, useless. I used the rearview mirror instead but didn't see anything.

I continued slowly, my hands gripped the wheel at ten and two. There! Something behind me moved. A glance in the rearview mirror showed a shift in the landscape. Two figures in dark clothes appeared and hurried toward me. No. Ran toward me. I jammed the stick shift back from neutral to first and pressed hard on the gas. I swore and the car made a sick grinding sound and then let out a sharp whine. Veering around a larger branch that lay over the right side of the road, I overdid it and turned too hard to that side of the road. There was a loud scraping rasp of thorn bushes as they caught the car, and tried to hold it back.

I snuck another glance in the rearview but couldn't see the figures. The steering wheel shuddered under my hands with a jolt as the car hit a deep pothole too fast. I gripped the wheel, slowed long enough to skirt most of another larger pothole filled to the top with muddy water. Signs of the storm were everywhere. From the downed trees to bark and branch-strewn driveway to the mud and saturated ground. Tree branches still glistened from the drenching rain and poked at the sky. Dark, matte gray clouds hung overhead, full of foreboding.

What time was it? I felt disoriented, suspended in both time and place. I guessed it was sometime around five. Maybe six.

Something moved on my left. My foot automatically eased

off the gas as I turned to look. Near the line of trees stood a deer, a large buck. I hit the brakes, my mouth slightly open. It stood and stared at me—directly at me it felt—before startling and bounding gracefully into the woods in two long strides.

Emptiness loomed in front of me. Distracted by the deer, I'd unconsciously turned in its direction. The driveway bordered a ravine, and the car was dangerously close to the edge. I jerked the wheel instinctively the other way.

Branches skittered along the doors, scraping against the fiberglass. Then I was back on the driveway. The car hit another pothole and the force snapped my teeth together. I screamed then, my hands scrambling over the wheel's surface as I tried to get it back under control. Tree branches and dead foliage spun dizzily, framed by the windshield.

Straight ahead, a downed tree lay across the driveway. The thickest part of the trunk was still in the woods, but its long, tentacle-like branches poked into the drive, blocking it. Slamming on the brakes, I tried to drive around it. There wasn't enough room. The front of the car crashed into the branches with a jolting thump and a crunching noise. A white cloud of steam spilled from under the hood, which was crumpled in the center.

I threw the car into reverse. Nothing happened.

Swinging the door open, I leaped from the driver's seat. The air outside was even colder than before. Like the steaming car, my breath came in great, white puffs.

I looked at the vehicle, heart thumping hard in my chest, leftover adrenaline making my limbs shake. Branches stuck out of the wrinkled hood. They had gouged at the right front side of the car, too. The dangling mirror had shorn off and lay in a puddle near the edge of the driveway.

Sickening fear pooled in my stomach as I assessed the damage. The car looked bad. Worse were the branches though—they were at least as thick around as my leg and lay halfway across the driveway. Maybe I could have maneuvered around them if I hadn't been distracted by the deer. But now, even if I could get the car out of the tree branches it was tangled in, there wouldn't be enough room to skirt them without falling off the steep bank at the side of the road. It pitched down and ended in a swampy area.

"No, no, no." The words hung in the still, cold air. I wanted to sit down and cry, or better yet, crawl into the backseat of the car and sleep. My nerves felt ready to snap, my body was exhausted and bruised. My head throbbed.

I climbed back behind the wheel. What was that old saying, "The only way out is through"? Well, that was my only choice here. I might not make it down the driveway, past this tree and its grasping, clawing branches but I had to try.

I put the car into reverse and strapped my seatbelt on. There was a flicker of movement in the rearview mirror. I glanced back instinctively. They were there. Four figures crested the small knoll. It was impossible in the pale light to tell who was who. They paused, momentarily still, and surveyed the situation.

A whimper slipped from my throat. I forced myself to ignore them, dragged my gaze forward, and started to ease the car around the branches. I sat up high in my seat even though it made my ribs burn painfully and craned my neck to try to accurately judge the distance between the biggest branches and the side of the car. The boughs screeched and scraped against the car's side, like giant fingernails on a chalkboard.

The car tilted too far to the left. I gave it a little more gas and leaned unconsciously toward the right as though my body weight would keep it from falling into the swampy ravine below. The wheel shook under my hands, bucking against the uneven surface. A screech of metal tore through the air. Then the car swung free as though a giant hand had pushed it from behind. I picked up speed. The car straightened. Glancing in the mirror again, I saw the two figures running after me. They became smaller and smaller. I luxuriated in the open space.

The driveway, really a private road, was longer than I remembered. It was bordered on both sides by tall grasses, shrubs, and saplings. I saw something familiar. The slight curve and an ancient oak tree that was missing its top.

The main road was just ahead. I could see it.

A shaky, relieved laugh escaped as I rounded the last small bend in the driveway.

I gunned the engine, barreling out onto the road and taking a hard left. Too fast. I should have slowed down.

I tried to counteract the motion, but it made the car veer crazily to the other side of the road. The mud was as slick as ice under the tires.

Everything moved in slow motion then. Tree branches grabbed at me. I screamed as the car veered directly into a boulder at the side of the road.

Chapter Thirty-One

The force of the impact drove me forward and then back in my seat. The seatbelt became a vice, digging into my flesh. My head was like a tennis ball whacked hard with a racket. My arms flew up instinctively to cover my face.

I closed my eyes. Behind the lids, I saw images I'd tried so hard to block out for the past two years. Shattered glass sparkling on the wet pavement. A tire running in a wobbly line down the road on its own. Nonna's arm, flung in my direction as though trying to keep me in my seat. It had been covered in blood.

Then, I hadn't had time to process what was happening. There had been an eerie, unnatural silence after the explosive crash.

Now, sounds filled the air, deafening me. My screams, the horrible screech of metal against rock, the popping shatter of glass breaking, as though a hundred boots crunched over the windshield. Finally, blessedly, the world was silent again. It was like the car had been filled with cotton batting.

Slowly, I removed my forearms from in front of my face. I stared at them.

Nonna's arms. Covered in blood. Her face—

No blood on my arms. A clicking sound came from under

the mangled hood of the car.

I didn't think my legs worked. I wiggled my feet but felt nothing under my kneecaps. I was afraid to look down. My ribs burned like fire when I tried to unclip my seatbelt.

The driver of the pickup truck stumbled out. Swaying on his feet. Beer cans tumbled out, bounced alongside his feet. He looked at them stupidly, then at us. He kicked at one of the cans, missed, almost fell.

It took three tries to unclip my seatbelt. Ignoring the pain, I reached down to touch my legs. The dashboard was crunched up against my shins. My fingers explored further. There weren't any sharp bones sticking out. No blood that I could tell. I pushed against the seat cushion with all my strength, which was about as much as a kitten's but couldn't get my legs free.

A bubble of hysteria formed in my throat and spilled out in a horrible, wheezing sound, full of panic.

The driver squinted at us in the darkness. "Help!" I tried to yell but it came out as a quiet croak. "Call an ambulance!" He stared at me a second or two, then swayed back toward his truck. Waves of dizziness crashed over me. I turned my head and was sick on the side of the door. "Nonna," I wiped my mouth on my shirt sleeve. "Nonna, don't worry. Help is coming."

A voice shouted, "Over there!" There was a far-off rustle of movement through the tall grass. The sound spurred my dull mind into action. Gripping my calves as hard as I could, I wedged them apart enough to find the seat lever. I yanked it. The mechanism groaned and the seat rolled back on its track. A horrible weight and pressure lifted from my legs. I opened the door; half fell out of it onto the rutted road beneath me.

The scent of pine and coldness filled my nose. It woke me

further from my stupor.

I plunged forward, following the road. At first, my legs were so numb that I fell once, twice, three times in quick succession. The feeling started coming back—tearing at my nerves with jabbing needles—and finally abated as the blood rushed back into my legs. I hobbled as fast as I could. A car. Just one car. One other person to come along, that's all I needed. I slipped and slid on the greasy mud underfoot but kept my balance.

Voices behind me. Feet running over dried leaves meant they hadn't reached the road yet. I glanced back, saw them. My heart leaped. They were much closer than I'd imagined.

My breath came in ragged, halting gasps. I kept running, a hobbled, erratic movement. I could feel them coming, hear their feet. But I couldn't look back. I'd lose precious seconds. And there was still so much ground to cover—

"Stop!" someone behind me yelled. It only made my legs pump faster. My lungs burned. There was a sharp stab between my right ribs. I wanted to double over, catch my breath, and sink to my knees. My arms flailed out in front of me, as my feet slid on the wet dirt road.

Don't think. Run.

I coughed suddenly, the dryness of my throat and the gasping breaths forcing air I couldn't spare out of my lungs. The animals in the forest—I wondered what they thought of the noise we were making. But then, they were used to it, weren't they? Prey caught in the darkness of the night. Screaming out in agony where no one can hear them. Their life ebbing away as a predator sunk its teeth into warm flesh.

The driver didn't climb back into his truck like I'd expected. He didn't root around, looking for his cell phone to call for help. Instead, he turned toward the ditch and unzipped his jeans. Swaying on his feet, he looked up at the stars and whistled Yankee Doodle *off-key.*

"Stop!" Again, the voice came from behind me. It was closer. They were gaining.

How much longer could I keep going? How long could they? My body wasn't cooperating with my mind the way it needed to.

How far to town? Until someone drove by and saw me?

The sob I'd held back turned into a cough. I gagged, wasted precious seconds, bent over, and prayed I wouldn't be sick. The feet were close behind me, slapping against the wet road.

Just a little further. I just needed to make it a little further. I'd been running for so long. I was so tired. But I couldn't stop now. I couldn't.

Legs like leaden bars, I stumbled over a small, downed birch tree. My foot caught a broken branch and I pitched forward. My arms outstretched instinctively to break my fall. My hands landed in the mud. When I stood again I was dizzy with fear.

The wind blew hard, a sudden gust that shook the trees nearest me, rattled the branches.

A wise old owl lived in an oak. The words from the childhood rhyme spun through my mind unbidden. *The more he saw the less he spoke. The less he spoke the more he heard.* What was the last line, I wondered dully.

". . . out!" The voice behind me was louder. Closer. What had it said? Get out?

No. Spread out.

I pulled myself up. Forced my feet forward. *Please, let a car come now. Please, please, please.*

The more he saw the less he spoke . . .

I'd never liked that rhyme. Goosebumps had run down my back and made me look twice, three times under the bed before launching myself into it. Trying not to touch the floor where the dark strip of emptiness lay.

I wobbled on shaky legs.

Run. I commanded myself. *Run.*

But all I could do was shuffle. My body was spent, energy gone. I shook so hard that the woods around me vibrated.

Ahead of me, through a tangle of vines smothering branches though, I saw something.

Lights from a car.

The road ahead stretched out like a river, undulating downhill. At the bottom of the hill, twin lights pointed in our direction. A beacon calling to me.

My legs were so heavy. I stumbled toward the lights. Toward safety. It wasn't that far. Just over the knoll and down the road a little further. Hope fluttered against my aching ribs. It wasn't far. I was nearly—

Hands clamped onto my shoulders. Such a hard grip, digging into me. Off balance, I pitched forward. Tried to scream as I connected with the road. All that came out was a tiny whimper.

"Get over here," Paula's voice was stern. I sank onto the ground. The hard hands jerked my arms behind me. Roughly, so that something in my back popped. I cried out again. I wanted to scream but couldn't find the strength. Gravel pressed against my cheek, damp from tears.

The last line of the nursery rhyme came to me then. *Why can't we all be like that wise old bird?*

The others gathered around me, I heard them but couldn't see them, and someone wound rope around my hands.

Then I was hauled to my feet. My right knee gave out. I sagged forward before being jerked up and back. My shoulders felt like liquid flames were being poured onto them.

"Shut her up," Venetia's voice commanded. Something dry was stuffed into my mouth. Around me, the figures breathed hard. Dizziness like a drenching ocean wave crashed over me.

"We need to get out of here. Get her off the road. Hurry . . ."

Chapter Thirty-Two

Voices muted as though underwater. I struggled to open my eyes but couldn't. Words came, fragments of sentences as I fought to the surface of consciousness.

"... can't have ..."

"don't think. .."

"... no. There's. . . risk ..."

Then I drifted under again. Grateful that darkness meant no pain or fear.

***

An orange glow behind my eyelids. Even in sleep, I squinted against it, tried to turn my head. Doing so created an arc of lightning down the back of my skull and into the top of my spine. I gasped. The fiery pain hopped to my ribcage where it felt like butter knives were being jabbed. A groan—from me?—and then the sound of rustling fabric.

I struggled to get my bearings. Where was I? The hospital?

I turned things over in my mind: the forest. Car accident. The road. The figures in the darkness. I must have been saved. Because why would they have brought me back to the Retreat Center? Why not have killed me and left me in the woods?

I struggled to sit up.

"Take it slow, Flora," a warm voice said from above my shoulder. "You've had a hell of a night."

Dread pooled in my belly as I recognized Randi's voice. *No, no, no.*

I groaned.

"You must be thirsty." A hand, cool on the back of my neck. It tipped my head gently forward and then there was a cool, liquid velvet on my lips. Despite myself, I sucked at it greedily, choked, and sucked again. Not water. Something sweet and a little bitter at the same time. I tried to open my eyes and see what it was but couldn't summon the energy.

"Slowly," Randi said. "There's plenty but you don't want to overdo it."

I tried to slow down but my body screamed at me to *drink, drink, drink!* Some of the liquid spilled down my chin and meandered in itchy paths to rest on my collarbones. When I'd emptied the glass, she gently replaced my head.

"Better? Elderberry juice is known to be a powerful immune booster. You could use that right now."

With effort, I opened my eyes. The room was dim. I was lying in a bed—but didn't recognize the room I was in. It was cold here, and dampness filled the air and coated my face and hands. Around the room were three dark shapes. Other people? I squinted but couldn't tell. Where were we?

Candles on the walls provided the only light. Randi was seated near the head of the bed. She smiled at me encouragingly when I glanced at her. My vision cleared a bit. Beyond her stood Venetia. Gwen was closest to the door—a thick, steel thing with three locks in a row along the frame. She looked like a woodland sprite that had been in a terrible storm. Her hair, shorn close to the scalp, made her fine features stand out even more. There were dark circles underneath her eyes. Her dress was splattered with mud and a couple of small twigs stuck to the hem. She didn't look at me but stared across the room at Venetia.

"Where . . . am . . . I?" My voice was little more than a croak.

"You're safe." Randi adjusted the edge of the bedsheet. "For now. That's really all you need to know. That and the fact that you need rest. She's tired," Randi said to the others. "We should let her sleep now. Nothing is as restorative as a good sleep."

I evened out my breathing even though it made my ribs ache and burn.

"We should have someone by the door," Venetia's voice was quiet, flat. "We don't have much time."

They moved toward the door.

"There are three locks," Randi replied. "Where do you think she's going to go?"

"This is our last chance," Venetia replied hotly.

There was silence for a moment, and I felt their eyes turn toward me but kept mine shut.

"And we need all hands-on deck. It will be fine," Randi's voice was firm this time. Venetia sighed and said something too quietly for me to hear. Then three sets of feet retreated from the room and the heavy door swung shut. There was another sound. *Click. Click. Click.*

All three locks being firmly closed.

I forced my eyes open, looked around me blearily. I was so tired. But falling asleep now would be fatal. I had to get out of here. Or at the very least, find something to protect myself with.

I surveyed the room carefully, still unsure where I was. It was about the size of my small kitchen at home. The walls were cinderblock, and the only light came from a battery-powered lantern across the room. The floor was cement, or it looked that way from where I lay.

I pushed myself up very slowly. My body begged me to *please, please stop.* But I swung my shaky legs over the side of the metal-framed cot and wrapped my arms around my middle. I shivered in the dampness, the woolen blanket sliding free and puddling on the floor by my feet.

Strange. I was wearing a long, white gown made of some scratchy material. It was tangled around my calves, a tie fastened around my neck like an old-fashioned nightgown. I peeked underneath it, relieved to see I still wore my bra and underwear. My socks and shoes were gone though, as were the clothes I'd been wearing. I wrapped the blanket around my shoulders.

There wasn't much else in the room. No windows. A small table stood in the corner beneath the lantern, but it didn't look particularly sturdy. Still, maybe I could wrench one of the legs free? I struggled to walk to it, clutching at the wall like a drowning person. My body felt heavy, as though a dentist's leaded apron had been thrown over me. I blinked then squinted. The door on the other side of the room shimmered a little, undulating slightly. I blinked and it was just a door again, large and solid looking.

Feeling my way around the room by holding onto the wall, despair welled up in my chest. There was nothing here. No signs of an escape route and no other potential weapons but the little table and maybe the lantern itself. I walked to it and hefted it in my hand. It was light, made of chintzy plastic. I'd be lucky to kill a fly with it.

Don't panic. Think about what you're going to do.

But my eyes kept closing. I sank suddenly to the floor, too tired to stand. Resting my head against the wall, I shook with cold before slipping into sleep.

Chapter Thirty-Three

Scraping at the door. I opened my eyes, unsure how long I'd been asleep. The locks were unclicked one by one. The door swung inward slowly, only halfway before a white, bony hand gripped it, held it in place.

Gwen, I thought. She came to rescue me. A feeling of relief started at the top of my head and cascaded downward. I got up and stumbled toward the door. My legs weren't cooperating. They felt thick and heavy and stiff like tree trunks.

"Now, I told you that you needed your rest," a voice said softly. "But I meant in bed, not on the floor."

Randi stood in the doorway, her short white hair tousled, her face devoid of a smile. She held the door partly open. If I was going to do it—make a run for it, battle my way out of this room—this would be the only chance I'd get. But my body wouldn't cooperate. I blinked slowly and felt a tiny bit of drool trickle down the side of my mouth.

"What . . . what's happening to me?" My words were fuzzy around the edges. I swayed on my feet. Randi closed the door behind her, then gripped my arm with hard hands and propelled me back toward the bed.

"One of my herbal remedies. Don't worry." She smiled but it didn't reach her clear blue eyes. "It's not poisonous. At least, not enough to kill you."

Not yet.

"Whatsss it?" I slurred.

"Valerian. In the juice."She helped me back to the cot and dragged my legs over the side. I wanted to protest but couldn't make my voice work. My limbs betrayed me, sinking gratefully into the soft pad. I leaned my head against the pillow, the aching in my head and neck eased slightly.

"It will help you relax, keep you quiet. What a busy, silly girl you've been since you arrived." Randi sounded as though she was scolding a naughty toddler. "You couldn't leave well enough alone, could you?"

"You . . . killsh . . . Ruby." Alarm bells started zinging off in my brain. This wasn't right, wasn't normal. What was happening to me? I pictured all my bodily functions shutting down one by one.

"Ruby knew what was going to happen. It was her fate and she'd accepted it. Of course, in the end, she did run." Randi conceded. "But that was just a normal human reaction. Nothing we hold her accountable for." She pulled the blanket up over me.

Nothing they held her accountable for? *What does that matter,* I wanted to ask, *if she died anyway?*

"Ruby knew that it was her time. The Mother made it clear, and we all agreed, Ruby included. It was her duty. An honor. One of us had to let go and let in another, younger member of the group. The one that Mother had chosen." Randi pressed her lips together and shook her head. "We all faced the same fate. Every one of us. It could have just as easily been Paula or Venetia. Or me. But Ruby wasn't young," Randi chuckled. "Hell, none of us are. And she had a heart condition. It made sense that the Mother chose her. Don't you see?"

She nodded and continued as though I had given an affirmation. "It wasn't a painful passing. The dart you saw—you did see it, didn't you, Flora?"

I stared at her, unable to say anything or make my body cooperate.

"It was water hemlock—boiled down and deeply concentrated. It's the most poisonous plant in North America. We always have some on hand for pests," she explained as though I'd asked. "A quick dart, a little sting, and then a quick passing. Thousands of old people in nursing homes around the country wish for such a quick end, believe me."

I looked past her toward the door. How many steps would it take me to reach it? Could I get there before Randi?

"You're very weak," Randi said, as though reading my thoughts. "There's no point in running anymore. It's nearly time."

Time for what? I thought but the words wouldn't come out.

Chapter Thirty-Four

Randi sighed and halfheartedly adjusted my blanket again. It was getting harder and harder to blink. Now, rather than my eyelids feeling glued shut, it was a great effort to close them. I stared at Randi and she gave me a sad smile.

"None of us want this but it's the way things are. There's a rhythm in our little community, Flora. Yes, we're sheltered from the world but that comes at a price. We have beautiful acreage and grounds. We have a freedom that most people never get to experience. We're in charge of our destiny, but eventually everything—even freedom, must be paid for.

"I don't know how much you know about the Aztec culture." She paused as though waiting for me to respond, then continued when I didn't. "They lived much like we aim to—living off the land, in harmony with nature and in line with the seasons. We depend on the earth here, much more so than in most of the rest of this country. Eating for us isn't as easy as running to the nearest grocery chain five minutes away. We grow most of our food. If we don't do the hard work when it needs to be done, then we suffer later.

"I think the Aztec people understood that, even better than we. They celebrated the harvest and the abundance of the earth with Tlaltecuhtli. She was the Earth Goddess; did you know that? She was also called the Earth Lady, but I don't think that's as fitting. Her story was tragic actually." Randi leaned closer and lowered her voice. "There were two gods, Tezcatlipoca and Quetzalcoatl who came down to earth in the form of snakes. They saw Tlaltecuhtli seated astride the ocean. She was powerful—so powerful—that they mistook her as a monster. At least, that's how the legend goes. But really, isn't that how it always is with men? They hate a powerful woman. Anyway, these two felt threatened by her and tore her apart, limb from limb.

"Her dismembered body became features of the earth: her skin grass and flowers, her eyes springs, her nose the smaller mountains, and her mouth caves and rivers. Then the gods tore her torso in two, the lower becoming the earth and the upper the heavens.

"The Aztecs believed in the power of Tlaltecuhtli and they saw great reward for worshiping her. Their empire became one of the greatest that ever existed on the continent of South America. Its influence is still felt today, isn't it?"

Again, Randi went on without me saying anything.

"But you want to know how all of this ties into our little community here." Randi squinted at me, then nodded as though she'd decided. "We're all so self-centered today. Always wondering about how things relate to us, how we fit into the picture. I bet you want to know what Tlaltecuhtli means to us. To Idyll Weiss." She rubbed her hands together, the sound was a dry rasp in the small space. "I'll have to give you the Cliffs Notes version, Flora. Our time is running out." She smiled and blew her bangs out of her eyes. "We're an agrarian community. And without the Mother's power, we would be not only very hungry but destitute. She gives us what we need to survive—to thrive even—and we give back what she asks when she asks for it."

I wanted so badly to blink. To look anywhere but Randi's face. But I couldn't.

She leaned closer. "Every time Mother asks, we provide her with what she needs. New life."

How?

"New life from existing life. Mother gets hungry too, my dear, just like you and me. Her hunger can sometimes be fed with our offerings—corn, grains, even game we catch here—but there are times when it runs deeper. When it requires human flesh. And when she needs it, we provide."

The matter-of-factness of Randi's voice and the words were discordant. It was as though she'd mentioned something she needed at the grocery store, or shared a trivia fact while dancing naked through the dining room. It didn't fit. None of it. I wanted to close my eyes and realize that I was just dreaming. I had to be trapped in some sort of nightmare. It was the only explanation that made sense.

"And that's where you come in dear," Randi patted my cheek with her cool, dry fingers. "I'm sorry that it was you. To be honest, I'd hoped for Liam, but it didn't work out that way." She shook her head, smoothed her wild hair slightly with a hand. "A terrible tragedy. It could have been him if we'd been able to keep him alive. But Paula gets a little too rough. Doesn't realize her own power. She's been like that as long as I've known her. Always made the boys cry at recess, always showing off how strong she was."

Randi chuckled. There was a noise at the door. She turned her head and I stared where her face had been. From the corner of my eye, the door swung into my line of vision. Gwen stood in the doorway, dressed again in the white robe.

"They're ready." Her voice was soft.

"Gwen!" I yelled but the only sound that came out was a strangled mew, like a sick kitten. She didn't look at me, just walked toward Randi and around the other side of the cot. Together, the women hoisted me up. My legs didn't collapse under me because they never straightened, to begin with.

"Make a chair," Randi commanded. On the count of three, they hoisted me up between them, like the winning softball champ and we stumbled toward the door. As we left the little room, I wondered again where we were. Further ahead, a buttery-yellow light pooled at the bottom of a set of narrow bare-wood stairs.

"Should have had Paula do this," Randi grunted.

They balanced precariously on the stairs, one ahead of me and one beneath me, sidestepping upward—*one, two, pause, one, two, pause*—until finally we reached the top. Both women were breathing hard. The door nearest Randi opened without her putting a hand on it.

It was the icehouse, I realized. We must have been in the basement. The room at the top of the stairs looked like I remembered it except now it was filled with glowing candles, too many to count. The light was bright. My eyes watered, tears tracking down my cheeks since I couldn't blink them away. Paula and Venetia stood beside the wooden table, which had been covered with a dark red, velvet cloth. A candelabra stood on either end of the table, each filled with black candles. The flames dipped and wavered as the door opened but none of them went out.

"Some help, please," Randi said.

Paula crossed the room in three strides and took her place.

Together, she and Gwen laid me on the table. I stared up at the beams and battered boards of the icehouse.

Though I couldn't move my body on my own, parts of it twitched and jerked in spasms—my left pointer finger, then my right ankle, and then my head once from side to side. This hadn't been happening downstairs. Was the herb wearing off? Part of me didn't want it to. Whatever was going to happen to me—maybe it would be better if I couldn't feel much of it.

The women circled the table. Venetia stood at the end; a book spread open before her. It looked brittle and fragile, the pages yellowed and the text strange.

She closed her eyes and spoke in a whisper. "Mother, we are here, ready to do your bidding. Speak to us, Mother, and make your presence known."

Silence in the room, other than the sputtering of candle flames. Even the wind outdoors had died down, leaving an eerie silence in its wake.

"Mother, we bring you an offering today on this special day of your New Moon. We ask that you look on us, your daughters, with your favor and empower us to continue our work here in this place. We recognize your generosity, O, Mother, and look to you for sustenance."

Venetia had begun to sway, her voice becoming louder as she switched to a foreign dialect. It was the same as when they'd been here with Gwen. She raised her hands and let her head swing down, her body swaying. The other women around the table began to murmur, first quietly, and then more loudly. They were chanting something—in unison to what Venetia intoned.

Then in English again, "Great Mother, accept this sacrifice today. Quell your hunger with this blood. Use it to prosper you."

I wanted to scream but even my vocal cords were frozen. I stared in terror as Randi unsheathed a knife close to my face. The blade rasped against its sheath. Both were engraved with strange patterns and slightly blackened with age.

The knife's blade was at least ten inches and curved upward a little. A filet knife, I thought. They're going to filet me, like a fish.

Randi looked toward Venetia and nodded. The strange language started again and the women seemed to sway to the beat of an unheard drum. Randi raised her arms over my chest, directly over my heart, the blade of the knife glinted in the flicker of candle flames.

Chapter Thirty-Five

A crash. Something solid and wooden hitting something else. Then a resounding boom filled the icehouse. The women gasped. Half of the candles went out. Cold air swept into the space, fresh and sweet. Silhouetted in the doorway were two figures.

"Oh, my God!" One of the voices said. Female. Then, "Put the knife down. Now."

Venetia swayed on her feet, her eyes glazed looking and her cheeks bright pink. Paula was bent over the table at the waist, forehead resting on her hands which were splayed there, moaning. Gwen stood and stared stupidly at the door without moving. Only Randi reacted.

"Get out of here!" she screamed; flecks of spit flew from her mouth. The words reverberated in the small space. She waved her arms as though shooing away chickens or an errant cat from her garden. "Get out! You'll ruin everything."

Rather than turning and fleeing, the figures rushed into the room. The first one—George I realized—held a long, skinny pole in his hands. He pushed it out ahead of him, as though he were going to jab Randi with it. She was startled and jumped away as he came within inches of her. Thrown off balance, she lost her grip on the knife. It clunked on the wooden floor.

Venetia blinked sleepily, looking first at the ceiling then to the intruders, and then to Paula. She seemed to be coming to, shaking her head, and looking around her in a daze.

"Take one step toward her and I'll do it." George's voice was deeper than I remembered, every word crisp and authoritative.

"Don't!" The figure behind him said to Paula who'd tried to sidle out from the back side of the table. "Stay there." Imani pointed a thick-bladed kitchen knife toward Paula. "Stay where you are. All of you."

Venetia started to cry, the sound like hoarse laughter choked and dried in the room. I felt George's hand on my shoulders.

"Can you get up?" he asked quietly.

I tried to shake my head or tell him no, but my body wouldn't cooperate.

"It's okay. We'll get you out of here."

"Imani," he shifted back from me a couple of steps. "Take the blow gun." He held the long tube toward her. She hesitated, then reached for it with her free hand.

"If one of them moves a step in this direction, shoot them."

"You can't," Randi said and put her hands out pleadingly. "You don't understand. We need to complete the ceremony. If we don't—"

"Shut up. The police are on their way," Imani said.

The fingers on my right hand twitched and one of my eyes closed partway before popping open again.

George positioned himself close to me and drew my arms over his back, squatted down, and tipped my weight over his shoulders in a fireman's carry.

Imani looked like a Roman gladiator, the blowgun in one hand and the knife in the other. She leaned close to me and studied my eyes for a second. "Whatever they gave you shouldn't last much longer." Her voice was so gentle I barely recognized it.

"Don't worry, Flora. I won't drop you." George started toward the door.

The women around the table were motionless, other than Gwen who swayed on her feet.

"This isn't right." Gwen's voice was so soft I barely heard it over the grunt of George as he overcorrected his step. I felt myself slipping before he repositioned my weight. I wanted to close my eyes but couldn't.

I pictured the women charging us, wondered if George would drop me in the process. Everything looked strange from my sideways angle. The women's faces were pinched and as white as marble. Gwen stared at us, her eyes huge in her angular face. She was shaking her head.

"Please—" Randi said again and moved toward us.

"Shut up!" George yelled.

Step, step, step.

We were nearly to the door now, Imani making her way behind us, covering us so that none of the women would rush forward. How had they known I was here? How had they figured out what was going on? The answers had to wait. Cold air blew through the doorway. We were close, I knew it even though I couldn't turn my head to see. So close—

"Please, you don't understand," Randi tried again. "Mother needs this. She—"

The rest of Randi's words were drowned out as George grunted. His body pitched beneath me, like a ship caught in a sudden gale. He lurched to the right, spinning me around. Now, we faced the door.

"Go, go, George," Imani yelled.

I smelled sweat on his skin mixed with the scent of a piney aftershave or deodorant. We got just a few steps along the path before George set me down, leaning me up against a tree. Imani still guarded the open door. George jogged back to her, shoved the door shut and shoved a nearby rain barrel hard against the opening. It wouldn't keep them inside forever but would give us a few extra minutes head start.

Helping me to my feet, George and Imani lifted me between them and half-carried, half-dragged me down the little path back towards the house and outbuildings. George had the blowgun now; Imani still had the knife.

"Stop them!" someone behind us yelled.

George and Imani broke into an awkward run. Something wonderful had happened though. In those few minutes, the feeling had come back to my legs. I tested them, dipping my toes down to the ground, and took a few stumbling steps.

". . . canwalsh," I mumbled. My lips too, were unfreezing. I wanted to laugh and dance but instead tried to form more words. I raised my voice, pushed the words harder through my diaphragm. "Can . . . walsh."

"What?" George turned toward me.

"Walsh . . . I can . . . walsh . . . walk."

Imani glanced at me, then George, barely missing a low-hanging pine branch that nearly slapped her across the face. They pulled me off the path and leaned me up against a tree. I nodded. Slowly, I moved my head on my own.

"It's . . . okay. Leave. Me. Go get . . . help."

They exchanged another glance over my head. Imani's chest heaved. George's face was sweaty. Behind us, the women were pounding on the door and speaking in that same unfamiliar tongue. But no footsteps pounded down the path after us. Not yet.

"Leave me. Please . . . get help."

"We're not leaving you here, dummy," George said. "You're the sacrifice. You're what they want most."

"But we can't get away like this. She's too slow. Is there somewhere you could hide?" Imani asked George.

"The barn."

She nodded. "Okay. Do that. I'll head for the main road. Bring back help."

"What about . . ." my voice stopped, and I tried again. "The police?"

"I made that up." She sounded apologetic.

Disappointment squeezed my insides.

George started to say something, but Imani cut him off. "There's no time—just hide yourselves. I'll bring back help," she repeated.

George's brown eyes looked worried but he nodded.

Imani gripped the knife and motioned toward the house and outbuildings. "Hurry."

Chapter Thirty-Six

At the "v" in the path, Imani swerved left, toward the driveway. George and I went right, back to the barn where we'd taken refuge the night of the storm. Had that only been days ago? It felt like months. He held the blow gun in his left hand, shepherding me with his right arm.

I could walk, but my legs were like a newborn colt's, and I slipped several times on the wet leaves. George's arm was the only thing that prevented me from tumbling onto the decomposing peat.

The barn, washed in gray light when we entered, felt like an oasis. It was quiet here and had the same familiar smell. George hurried me to the ladder that led to the hayloft.

"I know this is going to be hard, but do you think you can get up there?"

I nodded.

"I'll stay right behind you. If you start to fall, I'll stop you from going too far, okay?" George held up a finger, pointing to the loft. "I'm going to put the blowgun up there. I'll be right back to help you up."

I wanted to tell him that I was drugged, not a toddler, but only nodded again. I couldn't believe they'd saved me. The knife had been within inches of my chest . . .

George's feet disappeared, and I swayed. If they hadn't broken in at just that moment—

His boots reappeared, then the wet legs of his jeans, and finally the rest of him, backing carefully down the ladder. Seconds later, we were moving up it. The rungs felt slippery under my feet, and I had to concentrate with every hand motion upward but finally made it to the top. I collapsed into a nearby pile of hay. A cloud of dust billowed out and I coughed, squinting to keep it out of my eyes.

"We should find a better spot," George seemed to be speaking more to himself than me. He surveyed the large open space, then nodded toward a pile of a dozen hay bales on the far right of the room.

"There."

I groaned as he helped me to my feet again. He settled me behind the hay bales, then finally leaned back himself, knees drawn up and the blowgun stretched across his legs.

"What . . . happened?" I asked. A sudden wave of fatigue washed over me. I pushed against it, forced my eyes open wider.

"You mean, how did we find you?"

I nodded.

"I got suspicious after Gwen disappeared. So, I started poking around a little. I kept thinking about what we'd seen that night at the icehouse. Wondering what it meant. But I didn't believe anything serious was wrong until last night. When you and Liam didn't show up again at the house, I started to worry."

"You heard us leave?"

George smiled. "I don't sleep well. I heard you guys in the hallway and got up to see what was going on. I should have followed you. I wish I had.

"I dozed for a while but early this morning I knew something was wrong. No one else was here—Venetia, Randi, and Paula were all gone. When I realized you and Liam had never come back, I woke up Imani."

George readjusted his position slightly. It was dark in the hayloft, but enough early morning light spilled in to illuminate his face.

"We looked everywhere—checked all the grounds but couldn't find anyone. But we hid in the woods when they were bringing you back. We thought you were dead. They brought you into the icehouse and I stayed outside the door until I heard them coming back upstairs. Then I ran back to the center—Imani got there just a few seconds before me—and we pretended we hadn't seen anything. When Venetia came in we asked where everyone was. She said that you and Liam had signed up for an early morning writing intensive, that Imani and I could do ours that afternoon if we wanted. And that the other instructors were doing morning chores and cleaning up from the storm."

A shiver ran through me, hard enough to make my teeth chatter.

"When she left, Imani and I followed her. First, though, we found some weapons. I'd seen where Randi kept the blowgun when she'd pulled me aside to ask questions about a piece I read. And Imani found the biggest knife she could in the kitchen. Then we went back to the icehouse. I can't believe this is real." George's brow was furrowed, his face childlike in the soft morning light.

"I know." I stretched out my feet. Finally, the feeling in my toes had come back. It felt good to have feet again instead of concrete blocks.

George dug around in his jeans pocket and extracted a wrinkled piece of paper.

"Here, take this."

"What is it?"

"In case something happens to me. It's my wife's contact information."

"Nothing is going to happen to you. We're going to get out of here."

George nodded and tried to smile. "Sure, I know. But just in case. I gave one to Imani too. I want Cynthia to know that I died a hero."

"You're not going to—"

"FLORA!" Someone—Venetia?—yelled my name. The sound was jolting.

"Let me see what's going on." George crouched and ran lightly over the hayloft floor to the wide-open space.

"Be careful," I whispered loudly.

"GEORGE!" The voice continued to yell. "We know you're in here."

There was a clanging sound then, like a pot being struck with a metal spoon. No, I realized, it was the sound of the old brass school bell ringing in a discordant peal through the early morning air.

"You can't hide forever," Venetia's voice had changed into a singsong. "We're going to find you. If you make it easy for us now and come out, we'll be easier on you."

I glanced at George. His face had lost all its color. I crawled to his side, tried to peer out of the hayloft door. He grabbed me, pushing me back against the rough wood planks. He shook his head.

"Don't," he mouthed.

"There's someone here," Venetia called. "If you come out now, I'll give you the chance to save her."

George closed his eyes, his shoulders slumped.

Without waiting for him, I shimmied down the ladder of the hayloft and stumbled to the front door of the barn. Peering through the opening where the door connected to the structure, I saw Venetia.

She had Imani.

Chapter Thirty-Seven

Venetia's arm was around Imani's throat, like a wrestler. Imani was not a small woman, but Venetia was tall and had an advantage there. She held tightly to the younger woman's neck though it looked like it caused a lot of effort to do so. I'd once seen a feral cat in my neighborhood play with a mouse before killing it. The look in Venetia's eyes reminded me of the cat. Imani bucked and clawed against the arm pinning her. But with a chokehold on her, she couldn't get leverage to fight Venetia off.

I ran toward the door but stopped. I had no weapon. Where was George with the blowgun? I turned, ready to run back to the ladder of the hayloft, but George was already crossing the floor toward me.

He motioned to the blowgun, for me to move. I pressed myself back against the wall of the barn, peering out through a slit between boards.

"Hurry." My voice was a loud whisper. "She can't breathe!"

George ignored me, taking his time and lining up the shot. I wanted to scream at him to hurry, hurry, hurry, but kept my mouth shut. If he was inaccurate, he might hit Imani rather than Venetia.

He lowered the blowgun. "I can't get a clear shot."

"Give me that." A voice snarled and a hand and arm shot through the open door. Paula's body followed it. She and George tussled for mere seconds before she got the weapon away from him. She shoved him hard, and he tripped over some loose twine, nearly fell before righting himself. She aimed the blowgun, first at me, then at George, and back again.

"Move."

We didn't ask which way. I looked toward Imani. Her head drooped and her body wasn't moving anymore.

"No, no, no," I whispered.

Paula shoved me and I slipped in the mud and fell on my right knee. She hoisted me up by the collar of my jacket and shirt like a kitten scruffed by its mother.

"Go." Her breath smelled of onions.

I walked toward Venetia. Randi and Gwen had been standing out of sight on the path to the icehouse. Gwen still looked dazed, with dark circles under her eyes. Randi raised her eyebrows at me when I made eye contact. I looked away.

"What are we going to do with them?" Paula walked around us to Venetia's side, the blowgun held loosely in her hands. She looked very comfortable with it. I wondered how long she'd been practicing. Randi joined the others too; the three of them stared at us. Gwen looked somewhere past George's shoulder, face as blank as a sheet of paper.

I should have felt scared. I should have worried about what the answer would be. Instead, I felt a dull acceptance. I was so tired. Every bit of me hurt. Part of me just wanted this to be over, whatever the outcome was.

George nudged me as though he'd read my thoughts. "You okay?"

I shook my head, my vision wobbly with sudden tears.

Paula spat on the ground, narrowly missing my foot. She smiled, exposing her teeth. How had I never noticed how yellow they were before?

Imani moaned a low, dull noise. *She was alive.*

Through the trees near the house, shadowy figures appeared. I blinked. Looked again. I could just make out the dark olive sleeves and pant legs with the telltale yellow stripes.

State troopers. Police. Help.

A tiny flicker of hope, like a moth, flitted in my chest.

Were they coming this way? *No, no, no.* I wanted to scream, and kick and cry.

They'd just entered the house through the halfway open door. I looked away from them. The women hadn't seen them, had their backs facing the Retreat Center. I had to keep their attention here until the officers came back out and saw what was happening. We were still too far from the house for them to see us easily. Everything in me wanted to call out to them but Paula would zing us with darts before the officers could get close.

I glanced at George. He stared at the mud underfoot, his lips moving silently.

"... missed the window of time," Venetia said. "But we can't dwell on that." Her voice was strong, confident. "We have three to offer now, instead of just one."

My chest constricted, thoughts tumbling over each other like water in a brook.

"Let's bring them to the house for now. We need supplies."

Not the house. They'd see.

She started to turn, motioning to Randi to help her with Imani.

"Wait!" My voice was surprisingly clear. "I . . . know we

don't have much time. That we've messed up your plans. But I would like to know more about, uh, her. The Mother."

George's head swiveled in my direction comically, his eyebrows raised.

Randi glanced at Paula who looked at Venetia.

"What could it hurt at this point?" I held up my hands in surrender. "I mean, who could we tell?"

Randi half-laughed, half-snorted, and shook her head.

Paula swore under her breath and passed the blowgun from one hand to another. She was strong, stronger than any seventy-year-old person I'd ever seen in my life. But there were two of us and one of her. Venetia and Randi, as far as I could tell, had only one knife between them. If we could wrestle the blowgun away—

"Fine," Venetia sighed through her nose and leaned Imani against a fallen log. "Three questions and then we're done."

I glanced at George. The tiniest upturn at the corners of his mouth told me he'd seen the troopers too.

They'd neared the front of the house now, their uniform colors more visible.

Just a little more time.

I prayed George would figure out what I was doing and help.

"Well?" Venetia sounded irritated.

"I wondered," George wiped his glasses on his shirt. "How the group here began. I mean, Vermont is a long way from South America."

"Paula's fifth great-grandmother was a founding member," Venetia said.

That wasn't the answer I'd expected.

"But you're the leader," George said.

If Paula was distracted enough, she might release her death

grip on the blowgun. I had to wait for the perfect moment. I glanced at her, trying not to stare at the weapon, then back to Venetia.

Venetia narrowed her eyes. "We don't have leaders here. We're all equal. We do, however, all have roles to play. Mother tells us what these are upon our initiation. And we respect each other's contributions."

I edged closer to Paula.

"Oh." George looked from Venetia to me then back again. "Well, so, Paula, your family has lived here all that time?"

"That's two," Venetia pointed at George.

I leaned slowly toward Paula. The blowgun was within feet of me.

Paula nodded. "The property has been in the family for centuries." Her voice had a note of pride in it. She wiped her nose with the back of her hand.

Only one hand was left on the blowgun.

I launched myself toward her. Startled, Paula yelped, drawing back instinctively as I came at her.

I didn't know what I was doing, had no plan. Just threw myself toward the older woman, hands grappling for the blowgun. Venetia swore and I heard, rather than saw her, move toward us. But then George was by my side. Three sets of hands on the weapon.

It was thick and smooth, slippery in my hands. If Paula couldn't get it close to her mouth it was useless. She growled, recatching her balance, and shoved me back hard enough my teeth snapped together.

"Help!" I screamed. "They're trying to kill us!"

Venetia half laughed and half snarled, her hands covering mine, prying my fingers away from the slender tube. I kicked her in the shins, hard, and she gasped but didn't let go.

Where was Randi?

Time seemed to turn to slow motion. I could see and hear fragments of things—the hands on the blowgun, the mud under our feet, George grunting hard as Paula elbowed him in the face.

Then something icy cold and sharp pressed against my neck. My hair yanked back hard.

It was Randi. With the knife.

"Let go or I will slit your throat." Her voice was so normal, as though she were asking me to pass the honey at breakfast.

I stopped moving but didn't let go.

Venetia did though, sweeping her long hair over her shoulders, breathing hard. Paula used the opportunity to slam the blowgun hard into George's throat. He staggered then tumbled onto the muddy ground and leaves underfoot.

I had trouble breathing. The knife tip was pressed into the tender spot where my pulse pounded.

"Now, why did you say that, I wonder?" Randi crooned into my ear, turning me back away from the fray of people and to a little bunch of birch trees. Her hand held my hair in a death grip bringing tears to my eyes. "There's no one for miles around you know. No one to hear you scream."

My mouth was so dry I couldn't swallow, my tongue glued in place. I wanted to cry out again and yell for the troopers, but only a whimper came from my throat. Had they heard me before? Were they running this way?

I couldn't die now. Not like this.

They couldn't win.

Paula kicked George in the stomach. When he doubled over, she kicked him again in the back. Venetia looked on with a half-smile as George cried out.

"Stop!" I screamed. "Help!"

Imani lay motionless.

Randi jerked my hair again. Tears streamed from the corners of my eyes in response.

Where were the cops? The walls of the old house were thick. Had they heard me scream?

"I knew we shouldn't have invited you. I had a bad feeling. No offense." Randi's grip on my hair loosened slightly. "I know you're—"

"Put your hands up." A voice boomed. "On top of your head. Now!"

I sagged with relief as another voice—unfamiliar but blessedly authoritative—called out from the woods behind where Randi and I stood.

"No—" Venetia swung around; her eyes as wild as her tangled hair.

"Hands up!"

Two officers emerged from the trees, guns drawn. An older man with a lined face and a young woman. They were the most beautiful sight I'd ever seen.

"You stupid, stupid people," Venetia's voice was so quiet I almost didn't hear it. "Do you know what you've done? This place is ruined. *You* are ruined."

Her eyes burned into mine.

"Paula?" Randi's voice sounded breathless.

Paula stood with her hands overhead. Her eyes were fierce, her gaze fixed on me and Randi.

Paula nodded once.

The tight grip on my hair loosened. The knife tip slowly moved from my neck.

George rolled from his stomach looking dazed.

It's over. It's over. It's over.

I collapsed onto my back, staring up at the jagged branches overhead.

Epilogue

Six Months Later

The café was packed with people—the snow outside had given everyone the same idea. Jazz music played low, and a gas fireplace added a cozy feel. The shop smelled of dry, acrid coffee and freshly baked cookies.

George, Imani, and I sat close to the fire at a table loaded with desserts and our mugs of coffee. George hadn't been able to make up his mind which dessert looked best, so he'd bought what looked like one of each. Nearly all were made up of chocolate. Most of them were untouched.

Sitting here with them felt surreal. We hadn't seen each other since that day, but we'd kept in contact by email. A writer's conference in Boston had brought each of us to the area. It only seemed right that we met. So far, we'd talked about everything but Idyll Weiss and what happened there. Agents, how the query process was going, and what workshops we'd signed up for this weekend: yes. Traumatic experience at remote Vermont Retreat Center: no.

"Did either of you follow the story?" I finally asked.

Imani's eyes slid away from mine.

"Mmm, yeah," George had just taken a bite of a brownie studded with chocolate chips. "I testified."

I nodded. "Me too."

"Not me," Imani straightened her already perfectly squared shoulders. "I don't want to think about it any more than necessary."

"I've been in counseling with my pastor," George sipped his drink. "Trying to process everything. He says I need to stop thinking about the 'why' and just deal with what happened. But I can't wrap my brain around it—what they planned to do with us. I mean, if the police hadn't shown up. They were going to kill us and then what? Hide our bodies in the woods?"

"Or in the basement with the others," Imani said darkly.

The state police had gotten a call from a neighbor about my crashed car and come searching for its occupant. I shivered thinking what might have happened if they hadn't.

After we'd been rescued, the property had been searched. The missing young woman Blue had told me about was one of seventeen bodies they'd recovered from the basement. There'd been a press conference. Some of the remains dated back to the end of the 1800s, when the cult first originated in Vermont. My stomach dipped at the thought. Mother, it seemed, had been hungry over the years.

Paula had been telling the truth about her family's long history with the property. It seemed that her fifth great-grandmother—or maybe it was sixth?—had been one of the group's earliest leaders. How an Aztec-inspired cult had ended up in the remote wilds of Vermont we'd likely never know.

"Maybe a fire." Imani's voice interrupted my thoughts.

I sipped my drink, a creamy dark latte.

"That would have hidden the evidence—well, us, I mean— and they could have started again somewhere else."

"They'd never have sacrificed the Retreat Center." George looked between Imani and me.

I shook my head. "True."

"They could have set a fire in the barn or another outbuilding, though," George said. "They could have made something up about why we were in there—that there was a special session about getting in touch with your inner farming muse or something."

I smiled and even Imani's face softened for a moment.

"I still can't believe it really happened," I said. "It seems so—"

"Impossible?" George asked and I nodded.

We sat silently then, each lost in our thoughts. Probably each thinking about what had happened after we'd left Idyll Weiss. Imani had restarted her work as a school nurse. It had helped, she'd explained, staying busy. Plus, the kids distracted her from going back mentally to the Retreat Center day after day.

George had returned home too but had been struggling at work. I'd told him it was normal, that the stress of everything had probably caused it. He'd said it was more than that. He couldn't get comfortable anywhere or concentrate unless he was writing. He was considering quitting his job and trying to make it as an author full-time. Cynthia was fully on board. I suspected she was so grateful he was alive that he could have told her he'd like to move the family to the Arctic and she'd have readily agreed.

Now, George swirled a spoon through his drink before glancing at Imani and me.

"What about Gwen?" he asked.

I'd just sipped my drink and took time to swallow.

"She's pleading mental incompetency," Imani's words were unexpected.

"She is?"

The last time I'd seen her, Gwen had been stone-faced and rigid as the officers had cuffed her alongside the others.

Imani sipped her drink. "She didn't do anything. Why should she be charged?"

George nodded and finally I did too.

"And the . . . cult?" My voice was nearly a whisper.

"Disbanded. At least on the surface." George raised his eyebrows. "But who knows who else might have been involved? Things came up in court—about how the group used to be bigger and more active. We should go back there." His voice was firm. "Later this spring. Make sure no one else is living there and trying to restart things."

Imani shook her head. "Count me out."

"Me too." I shivered at the thought. "I never want to see that place again."

We were quiet again for another few minutes. It felt strangely comforting to be sitting here with George and Imani. Even though we'd only spent a few days of our lives together, we were bonded. Would it be like that for the rest of our lives? Or would time fray the connection we shared?

"Idyll Weiss," Imani said. "Doesn't that mean peace or something?"

George shook his head. "It's the name of a flower that grows in the Alps. It means noble and white."

Imani and I stared at him.

"What? Haven't you watched *The Sound of Music*? Dot is obsessed with it. She dances through the house singing "I am sixteen going on seventeen . . ." even though she's seven going on twenty."

Imani smiled and pushed away her half-empty mug. "I'm going to go. It was nice catching up, but I want to see if I can meet one of the agents that are leading tomorrow morning's workshop. I have a question about my manuscript."

"I can't believe we never talked about what we're writing now," I said, glancing at the two of them. "What are you both working on?"

"Technology spy novel," George grinned. "Something completely outside of my wheelhouse. And it's been helpful, you know, doing something very different. What about you?"

I fiddled with the salt and pepper shakers in the center of the table. "I'm working on my grandmother's memoir. I've wanted to write it for decades but never thought I could pull it off. It's more than three-quarters done, which is hard to believe."

"That's cool. Good for you, Flora. What about you, Imani?" George asked.

Imani smiled and stood up from the table. "I'm trying a new genre like you, George. This one is a thriller. Set in a remote part of Vermont. About several writers who go away on a secluded retreat."

"Purely fiction?" George cocked an eyebrow.

"Mostly." Imani slipped her bag over her shoulder. "Mostly fiction."

9 781950 976232